MY MOTHER MADE ME!

Sharon Brain

Cover by David Craig

Scholastic-TAB Publications, Ltd.
123 Newkirk Road, Richmond Hill, Ontario, Canada

To Roger

Copyright © 1978 by Sharon Brain. All rights reserved.

Canadian Cataloguing in Publication Data

Brain, Sharon.
    My mother made me

ISBN 0-590-71309-4

I. Title.

PS8553.R34M9 1983   jC813'.54   C83-098637-5
PZ7.B72My 1983

3rd printing 1983   **Printed in Canada**

Contents

Mothers!

It was one of those hot summer afternoons when you begin to think that maybe you should have gone to camp after all. Steph and I were at Marna's. We had dragged her little sister's wading pool under a shady tree and were lying on the grass with our feet dangling over the rim into the cool water. We were talking about mothers.

Steph was complaining because her mother had started serving health food all of a sudden.

"I'm surprised she hasn't dragged us all off to a nudist camp. That's supposed to be very healthy too. Can you imagine a whole summer of yogurt and soybean bread?" she grumbled as she stuffed a handful of pretzels into her mouth.

"Mothers!" Marna agreed disgustedly. "Take a look at these shorts mine bought me yesterday." They were yellow with green trim around the legs and positively awful. "She's always buying me stuff like this, and then she's mad when I don't like it."

It was my turn. "You'll never guess what *my* mother did. She asked my cousin to come for a two week visit," I moaned, "and *I* get to do the entertaining. She seems to think that dragging someone around the hot spots of Amesbury is my idea of a good time."

Steph stopped eating for a moment. "Male or female?"

"Female. Three years older than us — and beautiful."

Steph crammed five more pretzels into her mouth. Silently we stared up at the blue sky and thought about the dreary summer that stretched before us.

Then Carlie arrived — on the run. That should have been enough to warn us that something was up. Carlie is chubby, and running doesn't look good on her.

"What's new?" Steph asked lazily as she let the water drip off her toes onto my leg.

"A disaster!" Carlie panted. "The worst!" Carlie tends to be dramatic.

"Spit it out," said Marna.

"My mother's really flipped out this time," Carlie announced. "She's off on another one of her crazy feminist things."

Steph giggled. "You mean she's going to burn your bra?"

Carlie glared at her. "Take a walk in the traffic, Steph." Those two are best friends, but they trade insults the way little kids trade hockey cards.

"She's going to make me look like a perfect idiot," Carlie went on.

"That wouldn't be too tough," murmured Steph.

Carlie ignored her. "She says I have to take up a sport."

"That's not a bad idea," said Marna. "It might do you some good."

"Are you kidding? Tell me one good thing about being the only girl in Amesbury who plays *hockey!*"

"You can't play hockey," I said. "There are only boys' teams in Amesbury."

"That's what *I* said," Carlie explained. "But my mother says they can't stop me from playing just 'cause I'm a girl."

"Nonsense," said Marna. "She must be joking. She can't mean it."

"She means it," Carlie said grimly. "She says the hockey league is for *everyone,* not just boys. But I can hardly even skate," she added with a wail.

"Come on, kid. It's not that bad," teased Steph. "It'll toughen you up. You know, make a man of you and all that."

Carlie started to smile. "That's very funny, Steph," she said slowly. "But if you think that's a laugh, wait till you hear this — when I left the house, my mother was on the phone talking to your mother. Before she's through, we'll *all* be playing hockey."

The grin faded from Steph's face. For once Carlie

had made the kind of impression she wanted to. We were completely horrified.

* * *

Amesbury is just crazy about hockey. Except for the middle of the summer, whenever you want to see someone you know, you go down to the arena. Everyone is there. All the boys hang around the snack bar or sit in the stands and watch the practices. They're there for all the games, too, and whenever they have a chance they're on the ice themselves, racing around after that little piece of frozen rubber and knocking down anyone who gets in the way of their perfect backhands or wrist shots or whatever.

But it has certainly never occurred to me to *play* hockey. I mean, if I were really athletic I might play ringette—though I'd have to drive to Barberville to find another team to play, and they don't even have any money for snazzy uniforms, anyway. The only girl in my grade who plays ringette is the coach's daughter. So it's not a really big thing to do in our town, if you get my drift.

But every guy in town plays hockey—and they sure wouldn't want any *girls* horning in on their game. After the game, sure. But during, we belong in the stands, not on the ice. That's why we all sat up and stared at Carlie. This had to be Mrs. Klee's worst idea ever!

"She means it," Carlie said into the glum silence. "But I won't do it. We'd be laughed out of town. We'd end up being outcasts like those parasites in India." I was too upset to point out that the word was 'pariahs.'

"She *can't* mean it," said Steph. "Who would we play with—the five-year-olds? Even they would be better than us!"

"She doesn't care about a little detail like that! Once she gets an idea, nothing stops her. She says it's unfair that the boys get to use the arena all the time, and that there's nothing for us to do but stand around and watch them play. She says we'll be pioneers. We'll start the Amesbury Hockey for Women Movement."

That made me stop and think. Pioneers get a lot of attention. Last year Sally Grach became the town's first garbage woman. She got her picture on the front page of the local paper, and just last month she married one of the other garbage people; so it all worked out pretty well for her.

I closed my eyes. I could see myself skating around the rink after scoring the goal that won the game. A cute, dark-haired boy was waving at me from the stands. After the game, he was waiting for me outside the dressing room. He kissed me on the cheek and picked up my equipment bag. "Great goal you got there, Gorgeous," he was murmuring.

"Get that ridiculous grin off your face, Jane," said Steph rudely. "It's not funny."

I came back to earth with a thud. I can barely skate. And even if I played hockey for years I would never look gorgeous in those silly short pants and shoulder pads.

"Hockey doesn't start till September," said Marna optimistically. "Maybe by then everyone will have forgotten about it."

"They're taking applications now," Carlie pointed out.

"Maybe your mother won't be able to convince anyone we should play," I said.

"Fat chance! My mother can convince *anyone* to do *anything*," said Carlie with conviction.

We sat there and thought of our mothers talking to Mrs. Klee. Suddenly I wanted to be home so I could have my say on the subject. "I think I'll be going," I said casually.

Steph got up to go too. Carlie just stared at the grass. I've never seen anyone look so miserable.

"Don't worry, Carlie," Marna said. "Whatever happens, we're all in this together." She looked right at Steph. "Right?"

"Oh sure, Carlie. We'll stick by you."

"Of course we will," I agreed.

Steph and I headed off together. "Poor Carlie," she said as soon as we were out on the sidewalk. "I wouldn't want to be her for anything."

"I don't see how she's any worse off than we are," I answered.

"My mother won't make me play hockey if I really don't want to," Steph said. "She even let me quit baseball after she bought my uniform."

"My mother really thinks Mrs. Klee is great," I said nervously. "But my father can't stand her. And he'll really hate her now—he's chairman of the hockey association."

"Well, he'll be on *our* side then," said Steph.

I left Steph at the corner and headed down the back lane. I had a great book waiting for me at home called *The Great Gatsby*. It sounds like the life story of a baseball player, but it's not. It's about a man who falls in love with a beautiful, blonde rich girl named Daisy. He needs lots of money so she'll agree to marry him. He gets it, but by the time he's rich enough she's married to someone else. He stands on the dock of his lonely mansion and looks across the water at the lights of her house. He's very romantic, but I think he is also a crook.

I'm not quite like Daisy. I'm a bit on the chunky side, though not nearly as fat as Carlie. My hair is mouse-brown and I certainly do not remind anyone of a flower. But I could still imagine someone turning to a life of crime so he could shower me with expensive things to prove his love for me.

My mother was in the kitchen as I came in the door. "I'm glad you're home," she said. "I've just been talking to Doris Klee. I want you to play hockey this winter."

Home Sweet Home

As I set the table for dinner, I let my feelings show by banging the dishes down on the table as hard as I could. That always irritates my mother. "Stop it, Jane," she called from the kitchen. "You'll ruin the finish on the table."

Isn't that just like a mother? Here she was, about to destroy my entire life, and she was worried about her table! Since I wasn't speaking to her, I simply banged the plates down louder than ever.

She came into the dining room. "Jane, let's try to handle this maturely. We'll sit down and discuss it with your father as soon as dinner is over."

I said nothing, but I did a lot of looking.

When Dad arrived home, he was in a bad mood. He walked straight to the TV and turned on the news, without a word. My mother gave me a look that said, "Leave him alone." Then she put on her best smile and brought him a kiss and a drink. She was obviously buttering him up — and it seemed to be working.

Dinner was quiet. We had my father's favourite things — ham and potato salad, and apple turnover for dessert — but he didn't even get suspicious, just more cheerful. After dinner, as she poured his coffee, Mother said, "Hal, Jane and I have a problem."

"You're not the only ones," Dad replied. "I have to go out tonight. I've called a special hockey meeting." I looked at Mother. She looked at her plate. "Have you been talking to Doris Klee lately?"

Mother tried to sound casual. "Why, yes. I was talking to her just this afternoon."

"Then I guess you've heard her crazy scheme. I hope you told her how impossible the whole idea is."

I kept quiet. Whenever I get involved in my parents' discussions, they agree with each other and turn on me.

"I did no such thing," my mother replied. "I did tell her it wouldn't be easy — but I like her idea."

"Not you too! You know how tight we are for ice time. There are already teams playing at five in the morning."

"That's no reason why the girls should lose out."

"That may be true, but that's the way it has to be for now. Maybe when we get another rink — "

My mother interrupted him. She tells *me* never to do that. "By the time we get another rink your daughter will be too old to play hockey. And *I* think it would be good for her. I've signed her application and I'm sending it off tomorrow."

My father got very red in the face. He pushed back his chair and headed upstairs to the bedroom. My mother followed him, and I heard the door slam. My parents think it's bad for me to hear them quarrelling; so they always shut themselves away when they're really mad at one another.

I sat and looked at the dirty dishes. It was my night to clean up, but I knew I wouldn't be able to hear the fight from the kitchen. It sounded as if my father was winning, but that was probably because he's such a great shouter. I've had enough fights with my mother to know that she may be quieter than Dad, but she hangs in there longer.

Finally there was silence. My father came stomping down the stairs and into the dining room. "Jane, do you really want to play hockey?"

"No, I don't! I'd be terrible. It would just be a waste of everyone's time."

He started to smile and gave me a hug. "That's my girl. That solves the problem in this house at least."

But just then my mother arrived in the dining room. "It does no such thing," she insisted firmly. "She *will* like it once she gets started. She's playing hockey this year and that's final."

That did it. My father stormed out of the house,

slamming the door behind him, and my mother burst into tears.

* * *

There seemed to be no way out of our predicament. It might not have been so bad if Mrs. Klee hadn't been involved, but as Carlie had said, Mrs. Klee could persuade anyone to do anything.

She's the one who decided that Amesbury needed a new library. One day she was down at the old one looking for statistics on the rate of inflation in Hong Kong, and when she couldn't find the information, she decided that something would have to be done. Before you could say, "Who cares about the rate of inflation in Hong Kong anyway?" Amesbury had a big new library.

Personally, I preferred the old one. You used to be able to take a book to the librarian and ask her if it was any good and she could tell you, because she had time to read every book herself. Now there are so many books that the poor librarian is rushed off her feet just keeping them sorted, and she can't begin to tell you if a book is great or lousy. Mrs. Klee thinks that's progress.

What I'm trying to say is that Mrs. Klee gets things done. When she talks to you, you begin to believe that she knows better than you — better than anyone — exactly what the problem is and what should be done to correct it. Then once you're convinced, she never lets you alone until you've helped her get what she wants.

That's what she'd done to my mother, and now my mother was working on me.

There was no sense in trying to argue with her. She went on and on about how much I'd like hockey once I got started, how great it would be for all the other girls in Amesbury, how much we would accomplish for equal rights — and so on. Once Mother gets going, she's a little like Mrs. Klee herself. When there's something on her mind, it spoils every minute of my day.

"Do you want orange or grapefruit juice for breakfast, Jane? Most athletes drink orange. I read that in the paper."

"Have you tidied your room? When you're a famous hockey player, I'd hate to have to tell the reporters that you were one of the messiest girls I ever knew."

My mother wears you down. Even when she wasn't talking about my playing hockey, you could tell she was thinking about it. After Dad stormed out of the house that night, she sat down at the table and poured herself a cup of coffee. She stared at it for a while, and then she sighed. My mother has a very long, heart-rending sigh.

"I just wish I'd had some of the chances you have," she said.

Suddenly I could have cried, I felt so sorry for her. After all, she had grown up long ago, without all the advantages of modern civilization. I felt like giving her a big hug and telling her that I'd throw my body to the wolves before I'd disappoint her. But I knew where that would get me — on a cold rink at five o'clock in the morning learning how to slam a puck into someone's face.

Mothers!

Who needs enemies?

I met Marna at seven-thirty that night and we started off towards the ball park where Steph and Carlie were meeting us. Marna wasn't any happier than I was.

"As far as I'm concerned," she said, "the worst thing about all this is what it's doing to Jennie. Now she thinks that she'll be allowed to play hockey with her friend George. I don't know how I'm going to let her down." Jennie is Marna's favourite little sister. She has three of them and sometimes she seems more like a mother than like someone my age.

"But, Marna, are you willing to make a fool of yourself just so Jenny can play hockey? Why can't she play ringette if she wants to, and leave you out of it?"

Marna frowned. "Because Jenny's hero is Ricky Vaive and Ricky Vaive doesn't play ringette. And my mother says if I don't see this through, Jenny will never get a chance to play hockey, ever. And besides, who would she play ringette with—there aren't any ringette teams in this town."

We headed down Queen Street. That's Amesbury's main street, but the only thing open at that time of

Bluebird Café. As usual, a squad car was ___ ront of it. Through the window I could see ___ Belmer sitting on his own personal stool ___ everyone who went by. He's one of our town police___en, a nice enough guy, but a bit corny. He loves to tell jokes and they are without a doubt the worst jokes anyone has ever heard. When a kid at school tells a really bad joke, we call it a Belmer.

As we went by he got up and walked to the doorway.

"Hi, girls. Off to the ball game?"

"Yes."

"Say, did you hear the one about the duck that walked into a restaurant and ordered a bowl of soup and quackers?"

Typical. No wonder it's hard to have respect for the law. We smiled politely and kept walking. Belmer got into his car and sat with his arm out the window, waiting like a spider for the next poor fly he could capture and entertain to death.

He hadn't cheered us up any.

"Stop worrying about Jennie," I said. "Think about yourself for a change."

"You just don't understand, Jane. You don't have a family to look after. It must be nice. If you want to read, you read. If you want to watch TV, you do. You don't have to worry about who's going to drown the cat or fall into the toilet. You don't want to play hockey, so you just say you won't. No problem."

"Yeah, but if I want a coke I can't send someone to the fridge for me either. I don't have three little servants always on call. And everyone in my house tells me what to do. I've never been able to order anyone to do anything." People think an only child has an easy life, but they're wrong. Two adults to one kid is not a healthy ratio.

We weren't the only ones heading for the park. On a hot summer night it draws all sorts of people. There were parents pedalling bicycles, with their little kids riding behind. There were old people heading for lawn bowling. Public school kids were racing around on their bikes, climbing the screen behind home plate, chasing each other, and buying bubble gum at the candy stand. The babies were either sleeping or crying. That's about all babies do, I guess. It's not much of a life, but then the kids my age don't do much of anything either. They watch the ball game a little and some of them watch the tennis matches, but mostly they just stand around and talk.

There was a group of them standing down by third base when Marna and I got to the park. Most of them were boys, all leaning on ten-speed bikes. I couldn't see who they were talking to, but I figured it had to be a good-looking girl.

We spotted Carlie. She was standing near the group, but you could tell she wasn't part of it. No one was paying any attention to her. They must have noticed she was there, though — Carlie isn't the kind of person you could miss, especially when she wears that awful fluorescent orange T-shirt.

As Marna and I got closer, we saw her tap one of the boys on the shoulder and say something to him. He answered her, and then turned his back on her as fast as he could. I saw him glance at her and say something to the guy beside him. The other boy laughed.

Carlie saw us and came over.

"Hi. I was just talking to Steve Barrochuck. Don't you think he's cute? He said — "

Carlie has a knack for not knowing when she's not wanted. I think that helps her to stay friends with Steph, but it doesn't help much where boys are concerned. No matter how many rotten things they say to her, she always comes back for more.

Once Joe Watson, who thinks he's a real comedian, asked her to meet him at the library to help him work on a project. She was so excited, you'd have thought it was a real date. Of course he never showed up. The next day she asked him where he'd been and he told her he had decided not to do his project on elephants after all, so he didn't need her help.

She cried for about two days over that, but she didn't learn a thing. She still thinks that if she tries hard enough some guy is going to fall for her. Steph keeps telling her that until she does something about her fat body, her awful clothes, and her obnoxious personality, she'll never get a guy. Steph is not what you would call tactful.

You've got to feel sorry for Carlie. She's got that awful mother of hers, ten extra kilograms, and a friend who's always telling her she's stupid and ugly. No wonder she cries a lot. I like her, but sometimes I wonder if I should spend so much time with her. Maybe all the guys think I'm creepy too because I'm her friend.

The group by third base started to split up and I could see who the boys were talking to. It was Sandra Stephans. I wished I had brushed my hair. She's in my grade, but she looks at least nineteen. That night she had on a strapless tube top and there was no question about what was holding it up.

My mother says Sandra flaunts herself, but the boys don't seem to mind. They practically wait in line to talk to her. She has a boyfriend in grade twelve, and I don't see why she has to come down to the park without him and ruin everyone else's night. But then, Sandra Stephans is big stuff. Last spring she went to the prom and next year she'll be a cheerleader. She's a basic pain in the neck.

The funny thing is that she and Steph are friends. Not real close, but friends. They do projects together, and Steph sometimes talks to her in the halls. Steph says Sandra is lonely because she doesn't have any girlfriends. I can't imagine why she would want them when she has every boy in school panting after her.

Steph also says that Sandra has a quality brain. It hardly seems fair. With what she has below her neck, she could get by with nothing above.

Sandra walked by the four of us. "Hi," she said to Steph. "Playing tennis tomorrow?"

"Sure. Want a game before the lesson?"

"Great." Sandra smiled. "See you at nine." She walked on.

"What do you want to play tennis with a snob like her for?" asked Carlie.

"I want to play with someone who's good. Besides, she's no more stuck up than you are."

Steph says the weirdest things sometimes — and knows the weirdest people. She's really a bit strange herself, I think. She still takes piano lessons, not because she has to, but because she wants to.

Her hobby is raising goldfish and cats. She says she's teaching them to live together in harmony. Her other hobby is nagging Carlie.

The baseball game was over, though I didn't have the faintest idea who had won. As the players left the field, the little kids went running out to take over. Marna's sister Jennie found a ball and went to the pitcher's mound. A boy came and tried to shove her out of the way.

"I was here first," she said, pushing him back.

"Get lost," he replied. "Don't you have any dolls to play with?"

"Yeah," she answered. "I've got one at home that's just like you — with sawdust in its head."

They shoved each other again. Marna stood watching. "Come on, Jennie. Time to go home," she called.

The boy turned towards us. Jennie gave him a last shove that he wasn't expecting and he sprawled to the ground. Jennie grabbed the ball and took off with it. "Have a good game, Sawdust Head," she shouted over her shoulder.

"That girl doesn't need any help from us, Marna," I said. "She'll manage on her own."

"Maybe," Marna agreed. "But she sure wants to play hockey this year."

Carlie was watching Steve Barrochuck leave, hoping he would notice her and say something on his way out. He didn't look her way.

"Don't stand there with your eyeballs hanging out," Steph taunted.

Carlie's bottom lip quivered.

"And blubbering won't get you anywhere," Steph added. They headed off down the street together, Steph nagging, Carlie starting to get mad.

"Why do those two put up with each other?" asked Marna. "Steph is so horrid."

"Maybe Carlie is used to it. That's just what her mother is like," I said.

"You'd think Carlie would want a break, then. I don't know why they stay friends."

I laughed. "You know what they say: with a friend like that — "

"Who needs enemies!" finished Marna. "Beats me. Let's go home."

Some outside help

"If my mother doesn't get off my back, I'm running away," said Carlie the next day. The four of us were in Marna's yard again. "I can't stand it any longer. It's just like living with Steph."

"That's the most insulting thing you have ever said to me, Carlie Klee," snapped Steph. "I'm not at all like your mother."

"You are so," said Carlie. "She never lets me alone either. You both nag, nag, nag from morning to night."

"At least no one else knows about this yet. My dad says that the hockey association wants to keep the whole thing quiet until they decide what to do," I said, to cool things down. "They don't want the newspaper to get hold of the story."

"Mother says she'll give them two days to make up their minds. Then she's going to call the CBC," announced Carlie.

"I've never been on TV," said Steph. "Would we go

coast to coast?"

"She'd make sure they interviewed her, not us."

"What gave her this brainwave anyway?" asked Marna.

"She was reading an article by an American tennis player who said that sports are part of the cultural mainstream and that girls need to feel part of it," Carlie answered.

"Why can't she just work on her own daughter's mainstream and leave ours out of it?" said Steph. "Our mainstreams are no concern of hers, and she'd have her hands full enough with yours." Steph had lost her tennis game and it hadn't helped her disposition any.

Carlie ignored the comment. "My father's mad at her too," she said. "They had a big fight about it last night."

"Who won?"

"Don't know. It's not over yet. My mother called him a dumb jock and said that girls had bodies for more than one reason. After that, they made me leave the room."

Steph looked at her. "Don't eat that potato chip. If you weren't so overweight, none of this would have happened."

Carlie's hand stopped a short distance from her mouth. "It just so happens that I've lost over two kilos in the last two weeks," she retorted.

Steph laughed. "Good news," she said, eying Carlie's rear end. "I just found them."

"Come on, Steph," pleaded Marna, "stop fooling around. We have to figure out how to change our mothers' minds before it's too late."

"Let's have Carlie go on a hunger strike," Steph suggested. "That'll solve two problems at once."

"The next time you go to the dentist, I'm going to ask him to wire your jaw shut," shouted Carlie.

"Will you two quit it! You sound just like my parents." I was getting tired of the whole thing.

"Let them fight," said Marna. "I don't think they could come up with half an idea between them."

"Oh sure," snapped Steph. "I suppose you know just what we should do?"

"If everyone doesn't stop crabbing at me I'm going to run away," said Carlie for the fourth time that afternoon.

Steph stopped and turned on her. "What did you say?"

"You heard me. I said if everyone — "

"Yes, I heard you," said Steph slowly. "I do believe a miracle has happened. The Chubby One has finally said something worth listening to."

"What is she talking about?" I asked Marna.

"Beats me."

"It's the answer," said Steph. "It's the only thing to do. We'll *all* run away."

* * *

Running away was the best idea we'd had so far, but

the next day we were still in Amesbury. As a matter of fact, I was in the back seat of the family car on the way to the train station to pick up Allison, my cousin from Chicago.

My mother and father were in the front fighting, although they didn't say a single angry word. I don't know if all parents fight like that, but mine sure do. They were being perfectly nice to each other, but I could tell that things were still bad. Maybe it was because they were nicer than usual.

"Dear, would you mind very much not smoking that cigar in the car? You know it makes me feel a little ill."

"Of course, darling. You only need to ask."

That kind of thing.

I hadn't seen Allison since her family had moved to the States three years before. I did see the newspaper picture that was taken when she was Junior Prom Queen. It was pretty impressive. But I still wasn't prepared for what stepped off the train.

She was beautiful! She was wearing white denim jeans and a jacket that were dynamite with her long blonde hair. She was tall and slim and gorgeous, and all of a sudden I wanted to go and hide somewhere— like under the back wheels of the car.

Allison kissed my parents. For one terrible moment I thought she was going to kiss me too, but she didn't. "Hi, Jane," was all she said. Her smile was toothpaste white.

My mother took over right away. "How's your mother, Allison? She wrote that she wasn't feeling too well. And is your father over his cold?"

We got two suitcases in the trunk, but I had to hold the third on my lap. Allison was obviously as spoiled as she was beautiful. No one needs three suitcases full of clothes.

On the way home, Mother and Allison chatted about all the family news. In passing, Mother told Allison that I was planning to play hockey this winter.

Allison turned to me. "Oh? When do you start?"

"Never," I muttered.

Mother turned around and glared at me and I glared back. But since there was no point in starting the argument all over again in front of Allison, I kept my mouth shut. My father just drove, but he drove mean.

When we got home, I took Allison up to her room. She sat down on the bed and took a nail file out of her purse. Her nails were already perfect as far as I could see. I sat on the window sill.

"So you don't want to play hockey?" she said.

"Are you kidding?" I cried. "Do I look like a hockey player?"

"I don't know. What do hockey players look like?" she asked with a smile.

"They weigh a hundred kilos or so and have huge biceps and no front teeth. And they're vicious."

She laughed. "No, that doesn't sound much like you.

But your mother seems pretty determined. How are you going to get out of playing — leave town?"

My mouth dropped open. "How did you know?"

"What? You mean you really are running away? Tell me about it."

So I did, although there wasn't much to tell. "We've decided to leave," I finished, "but we can't think of any way to do it. We don't have enough money to go far, and we're afraid to hitch-hike."

"You're smart. Hitch-hiking is more trouble than anyone needs."

"We thought of going to someone's cottage, but that's the first place our parents would look."

"Camping out?" suggested Allison.

"We can't. When it's cold or damp, Carlie's feet swell and she can't walk. She uses an electric blanket even in summer."

"Doesn't sound as if she'll make much of a hockey player."

"Her mother says it's all in her head. So does Steph. That's what started their last fight. Now they aren't speaking to each other and Marna and I have to relay their insults back and forth."

"Are you sure it wouldn't be easier just to give in?" Allison asked.

"Never!"

"Well, keep me up to date on what you decide."

We talked a little more while Allison changed into

bluejeans, which didn't make her look one bit grubbier, washed her face, which was perfectly clean, and brushed her hair, which didn't need brushing at all.

As we went down for dinner I told myself that if I took as much time to get ready to eat meatloaf as Allison did, I'd look pretty good too. But as I listened to her telling my mother what the man from the *Chicago Tribune* had said when he took her picture as Queen of the Junior Prom, I knew that three hours in front of the mirror wouldn't accomplish for me what three minutes had for Allison.

After dinner I cleared the table while Allison went upstairs. My mother was in the kitchen cleaning up. "How are you two getting along?" she asked when I came in with the glasses.

"How should I know?" I snapped.

"She's a nice girl."

"Handsome is as handsome does," I muttered, picking up a dish towel. My mother says that to me all the time when I complain about my looks.

"Yes, she is pretty, isn't she? She looks like our side of the family."

That was a riot. I'm supposed to look like our side of the family too; so there was obviously something wrong somewhere. "Lucky she doesn't have to play hockey," I muttered. "She wouldn't look half as good with false teeth."

My mother smiled sweetly. "Why don't you ask her about that, Jane?"

"We've already discussed it," I said stiffly. "She feels the same way I do. She thinks hockey's dumb too — and that no girl in her right mind would play it."

"Really?" She looked surprised.

"Yes, really! And if you — " But I didn't finish because Allison came in. I didn't want to have a fight with my mother in front of her. I didn't really know her well enough yet.

My mother must have agreed. "I'll finish the dishes, girls. You run along and enjoy yourselves tonight. Tomorrow it will be your turn."

I didn't argue. We left quickly, before she changed her mind.

As we walked down Queen Street, I could hardly believe this was the same town I was in the night before with Marna. Last night no one had even seen us. Tonight guys were crossing the street to say hello.

"I don't usually get this much attention," I said.

"I do," Allison replied. "Sometimes it's a real drag, but I guess that's what you get . . ." She trailed off, but I knew what she meant: ". . . for being gorgeous" was the rest of the sentence. And she *was,* but she wasn't supposed to say it. Besides, if she didn't want to be beautiful, why did she work at it?

"I guess that sounds conceited," she went on, "but I try to be realistic about the way I look. Sometimes I feel as if I'm walking around behind someone else's face and everyone is smiling at it and talking to it and not paying any attention to the me behind it."

Strangely enough, I knew what she meant. Sometimes I look in the mirror and see a little round face, scrawny brown hair and big brown eyes and I think, Who is that creepy kid anyway? I'm really tall and slim, with long eyelashes, blonde hair to my waist and a deep golden tan that stays all year. As a matter of fact, I think that behind the creepy mask I wear I really look a lot like Allison. It dawned on me that maybe behind her mask she really looked like me, and that made me laugh.

"What's so funny?" Allison asked.

"Nothing. I was just thinking that maybe that's my face you have on — and I'd like it back now, please."

Then she laughed too. She wasn't so bad after all.

We left Queen Street and headed for the park. There was a bunch of kids sitting on the swings in the playground. Carlie and Steph and Marna weren't around, but Bill Graydon was. He waved and we walked over.

Bill and I started kindergarten together. As far as I know, he's never told anyone about the day I wet my pants on the way home from school, and I've never told anyone that he came over to my house and cried the day his grandmother died. We've always known each other pretty well.

"Sit down," he said, offering us part of his teeter-totter. "Constable Belmer's on the evening shift this week, so we're going to give him some exercise."

"What do you mean?" Allison asked.

After I'd introduced them to each other, Bill told her about the alarm system in the arena. The Town Council put it in after a team from up north broke in and wrecked the arena last year. The team said in court that they had done it because the referee was biased, but the judge wasn't impressed. The fine they had to pay was used to buy an expensive alarm system. It goes off when anyone pushes or pulls on the windows. Then a police car races up with sirens blaring, and one of the policemen runs around the arena trying to catch the vandals who set off the alarm. Generally the kids don't fool with the alarm except when Constable Belmer is on duty. They figure he needs the exercise.

It was getting dark, but the guys in our town seem to have radar where pretty girls are concerned. Soon there were five of them standing around talking to Allison about the Chicago Black Hawks. She knew a lot more about her home-town team than I would have.

I sat there feeling the cool breeze in my hair. I felt pretty good. Because I didn't look like Allison on the outside, I didn't have five boys talking to me; but I knew I looked a lot like her on the inside. It was just their tough luck that they couldn't see it.

I glanced at Bill. He was watching me, but when he

saw me look at him, he shifted his eyes and stared at the tree over my head. Maybe it was just the shadows from the street light, but all of a sudden Bill didn't look like the boy I had always known. He looked different, more special.

When I continued to look at him, he coughed. "I'll be glad when summer's over," he said.

"Why? Don't you like your job?"

"Yeah. But there's a special hockey camp in September that I'm going to."

My nice feeling disappeared. Hockey again. I tried to smile.

"Maybe you could come and see some of my games this year," he said. "I mean, if you're not busy or anything."

I wondered how fast he would change his mind when he found out he might have to give up some of his ice time for me, or worse yet, play on the same team.

Just then the burglar alarm went off. I jumped, and then tried to pretend I hadn't been startled. Two more boys slipped into the playground. One was Bill's older brother, Darryl. They were puffing a bit from their run.

Almost immediately we heard the siren.

"Not bad," said Darryl, looking at his watch. "Thirty seconds. That must be a record."

"Very efficient," said Allison.

Darryl looked at her. "Who are you?" he asked.

They started to talk. I watched Belmer struggle out

of his car and hurry to the door. He made sure it was locked, then he chugged off to check around the outside of the arena. It's a big building and it took him quite a while. When he got back, he pulled out some keys, unlocked the front door and went in, closing it carefully behind him.

We all got up to leave. We knew if we were still there when he came out he'd ask us all kinds of questions. Then he'd rant and rave about the penalty for public mischief and send us home.

Somehow, Darryl and Bill ended up walking home with us. Darryl and Allison were talking about the arena and its new alarm system. It was a very boring conversation. Bill spent the time giving me the gory details of a book he was reading about the headhunters of New Guinea. By the time we got to my front door, Allison and Darryl were far behind.

"My family is going to the lake tomorrow," Bill said.

"That's nice."

"I heard Darryl ask Allison if she wanted to go."

Allison had been in town for three whole hours and she had a date already. I felt horribly depressed. Then I realized that Bill was saying something more.

"So I guess you might as well come too," he muttered, looking at his shoes. Before I had time to answer, he was gone.

I had a date — a real, live date. It wasn't a very romantic invitation, but it would do. Bill's problem was he had been reading too many cannibal books and not enough romances. I decided I was just the kind of girl he needed. How could I get him to read *The Great Gatsby?*

I flew up the stairs and threw myself on the bed. Suddenly I remembered my chin. I ran to the mirror. There it was, bigger and redder than ever. I realized that if it hadn't been dark Bill wouldn't even have talked to me. But in the bright sunshine tomorrow . . . I looked at the pimple and wondered if I could cover it with make-up. That might work as long as I didn't go swimming. Then I heard Allison coming up the stairs. She'd know what I should do.

"Perfect," she said to me, before I could say a word.

"What? Darryl?"

She sat me down on the bed and said in a whisper, "Of course not. He's okay. But my plan — it's perfect. I know how you can run away."

The perfect solution

That Allison really has a brain. All the time she had been talking to Darryl, she had been hatching a plan so simple, yet so brilliant, that Nancy Drew would have been proud of it. I woke up at nine o'clock the next morning and called everyone to tell them to meet me at Marna's. No one was too pleased at being routed out of bed so early, but they were all there.

Allison had given me ten minutes to prepare them.

"Can we trust her?" asked Marna.

"I don't think you should have given away our whole plan to a complete stranger," Carlie added.

Steph snorted. "Listen to this! Our whole plan! Maybe someone could ask Miss Electric Blanket just what our whole plan is? Perhaps she has managed to come up with something brilliant between chocolate bars."

I stood firm. "Well, I trust her. And if we don't do something soon, before we know it we'll be down at

Benson's Sports Store buying mouthguards."

When Allison arrived, the girls were still hostile, but in five minutes she had them convinced. They would have run away to the moon if she'd suggested it.

"I know you don't have much money," she began, "but you won't need any. You'll only need sleeping bags and food. You'll be close to home, but you won't be discovered until you're ready to come back."

"Sounds great," said Steph. "Tell us quick."

Allison smiled. "Figure it out for yourself. It's the one place where no one would ever guess you'd hide to run away from hockey."

I couldn't keep quiet any longer. "And the only person who ever goes there now is Constable Belmer."

Marna guessed it first. "The arena!"

"Right," said Allison. "You walk over there one night when everyone thinks you're in bed. You get in unnoticed. Then you're set with all the comforts of home. Showers, toilets, lots of room. Carlie can even take her electric blanket."

"What about the janitors?" asked Steph.

"I checked that out. They get all of July off," said Allison.

"And the alarm?" asked Marna.

"It'll still go off. We can't stop it, but it won't be a problem. Darryl Graydon told me there's a window . . ."

I stopped listening. We had gone over the plan several

times last night, and it was foolproof. I started thinking about Bill instead. My chin didn't look one bit better this morning. The temperature was twenty-eight again, so I didn't think I could get away with wearing a cowl-necked sweater. Too bad. I could have dropped my face into the sweater whenever Bill looked too closely.

When Allison finished talking, everyone was convinced. We decided we had wasted enough time. We would go the very next night.

"There's one other thing," added Allison. "Jane and I thought it might be a good idea for you to tell your parents that you've decided to play hockey after all."

"And then run away? That doesn't make sense," said Marna.

"Allison guessed that we were thinking about leaving town," I explained. "Our parents might have the same idea and be watching us pretty closely. This way we'll throw them off the track. We can write them a letter and tell them how to let us know when they've given up. Allison can say she found it under her door."

Everyone agreed. They wanted to start the letter right then. I got up to leave. "You go ahead without me. I have to go home and wash my hair."

"Why? Got a big date?" teased Steph.

"As a matter of fact, I do. Bill Graydon asked me to his cottage for the day."

Marna looked at me strangely. I guess she was jealous. She's never had a date.

"His brother asked Allison, so I'm going too," I added quickly.

"But, Jane," said Marna. Then she paused. "Never mind," she said quietly.

Allison and I headed off towards home. I was really looking forward to a day at the lake. No wonder Marna was jealous.

I found my mother and father in the kitchen drinking coffee. Since they were talking to each other in a friendly way, I supposed the fight was over — although I noticed they were staying away from the topic of hockey. When my mother went into the dining room, I followed her. I took a deep breath and blurted out the lie as fast as I could.

"Mother, I've decided to play hockey this year."

She looked at me with surprise, then smiled happily. "Jane, I'm proud of you. I know it won't be easy, but one day you'll thank me for it."

That really did it! I was glad I was running away. Parents think they know so much more about your life than you do.

"Let's not tell your father just yet. It'll spoil his weekend. Is that all right?"

"Sure," I said.

I watched her leave the room, all smiles. I couldn't believe it. She was worried about spoiling Dad's weekend but she didn't mind destroying my whole winter. Sometimes I don't understand her at all.

When Allison came upstairs I was just getting out of the shower. I walked into her room with my head wrapped in a towel.

"Allison, what's with my mother? Why can't she see that I just don't want to play hockey?"

"Maybe she does."

"What do you mean?"

She shrugged. "It's hard to explain. Take my mother: we fight all the time. When she gives me advice, I ignore it. But sometimes she knows what I'm talking about even when *I* don't."

"I wish my mother was like that," I said.

"I bet she is," said Allison. "What have you been doing to your chin?" she added. "Leave it alone."

* * *

During the drive to the lake, Allison and Darryl sat in the front seat, laughing and talking the whole time. Allison was flirting like mad and Darryl was loving it. She needed his help for our plan, but I thought maybe she was going a bit overboard.

Bill and I spent a lot of time looking out the windows. We couldn't think of much to say to each other. We'd always been friends, but everything seemed different now that he was my date. I knew I was supposed to get him to talk about himself — that's what all the books say — but that would have meant hockey, and I really didn't want to hear more about that. I was afraid the news might have leaked out already, but he didn't seem to know anything.

The other problem was my chin. Allison had said the best thing to do was forget about it, but that's not easy to do unless the pimple is on someone else's face. Whenever I had to look at Bill, I casually brought my hand up to my mouth, but most of the time I just let him look at my profile. It's pretty hard to carry on much of a conversation like that.

Things improved when we got to the cottage. Mrs. Graydon gave us a sandwich and told us she'd see us at suppertime. I got into my bathing suit, lay in the warm sunshine and watched the others water-ski.

Allison took her turn after Bill and Darryl. She was great. She dropped a ski and cut back and forth behind the boat like a pro. Then she tried a turn-about on the trick skis. She fell three times before she finally managed it, but each time she just laughed and asked for another try. I would have died of embarrassment.

While the boys put the boat away, Allison swam to the raft and back. Then she flopped down on the dock beside me. "You should have come water-skiing with us, Jane. It's not so tough after the first time."

"No way! I tried it once at Steph's cottage. When I fell, I forgot to let go and swallowed half the lake before Steph's father stopped the boat."

"Well, I think it would be more fun if you did something besides just lying there. If Bill wanted a rug for his dock, he'd buy one."

I took a look around me. There was a croquet set on the lawn, as well as lawn darts and a volleyball net. There were bicycles in the garage and a basketball net fastened above the garage door. And I remembered Bill saying that if we got bored there was a golf course just down the road.

I groaned. "Don't boys ever just sit around and talk?"

"Not in the daytime," said Allison.

So when Bill came back to the dock I asked him what he wanted to do. His face lit up. "I wondered if you'd ever get tired of lying around. How about a canoe ride?"

I hadn't been in a canoe since I was at Camp Wanatachee four years before. It had rained a lot that week and my job had been to sit in the middle and bail out the water with an old tin can. It hadn't been much fun. But with Allison glaring at me, I just smiled and reached for a paddle.

After Bill taught me a few strokes, we set out for the island that was right across from the cottage. It was hard work and I was glad when we got there.

We beached the canoe and went for a swim. Then we lay in the sun and dried off. We talked about canoeing and Bill told me about the trip he had gone on last summer. He seemed like the Bill I had known before, not the stranger in the car.

"Allison's okay," he said.

"No wonder. Just look at her."

"Yeah, I guess that helps. But she's really fun to have around. The last girl Darryl had up here spent the whole day on the dock putting on suntan lotion. I kept hoping she'd get so greasy she'd just slide into the water and disappear."

Strange, isn't it? When I go to a cottage, I like to lie around and read magazines and talk about boys and clothes and stuff. But Bill thinks you're supposed to play games the whole time. He's going to make a great phys. ed. teacher or something.

On the way back to the cottage I worked hard at paddling properly. We docked the canoe perfectly.

"How'd she do?" asked Allison.

"She wasn't bad."

It felt pretty good when Bill said that.

I don't think I sat down for the rest of the afternoon. We played volleyball for awhile and then walked down to the tennis courts. I think I managed to hit the ball over the net three times in the hour we were there, but at least I kept trying. Bill was great. He tried to help me out but he never made me feel stupid. He kept saying I would get better if I played more.

When we got back to the cottage it was time for supper. I was so tired I could hardly lift my fork, but everyone was laughing and talking about Allison's forehand and Bill's great serve and I actually knew what they were talking about. I liked that too. All in all it was a super day, though it was a lot different from what I had expected.

After supper, Jeff Cranley arrived. Jeff is a friend of Darryl's. He's very big around school — he's captain of the basketball team and would probably have been elected president of the student council except the guy who was supposed to be running his campaign quit school before he got around to making any posters.

Jeff drove up in his father's sports car. He brought a girl with him, Janet Klaski. She had been in my French class for a while, but I didn't know her very well. She had moved to Amesbury only three months before. I couldn't understand what Jeff was doing going out with her. She was too young for him and she wasn't any prettier than I was. It seemed strange to see them together.

After he introduced her to everyone, he gave her a long kiss. Then he told her to run and get him a coke. She went off with a big smile on her face.

"I sure know how to make 'em happy," he said to Darryl.

Judging from the look on Allison's face, she wasn't too impressed with him, but Janet sure was. I could understand that. To tell you the truth, I was a little envious. Bill was nice and everything, but he was hardly in Jeff Cranley's league. Compared to Jeff, he was just a kid.

We lit a bonfire and sat around talking. Actually, we spent most of the time listening to Jeff. He knew funny stories about all the teachers and he sat there with his arm around Janet, talking about school and his summer job and his plans for the following year. Nobody else did much talking, but that didn't bother Jeff.

Finally Darryl looked at his watch and said it was time to start for home. We said goodbye to Jeff and Janet, and Darryl and Allison walked them to their car.

Bill and I decided to put out the fire. We went down to the lake with a bucket. The stars were shining on the dark water and I could hear someone singing from across the lake.

"I wish we didn't have to go back," said Bill. "This is the best time of the day."

"It's so quiet," I agreed.

"Some nights I come down here to sit and think. I always wish I had someone to talk to then."

"What about?"

"Everything. But I guess you never find someone you can talk to like that." He stopped and looked at me. I felt everything stand still. He put his hand on my shoulder and he kissed me.

His face was warm and fuzzy, and mine felt soft and cool on his. It was a moment I wanted to hold in my hands forever.

Then we heard Darryl and Allison coming back. We both bent down to pick up the bucket, and our heads bumped together so hard I almost fell off the dock. He grabbed me just in time. We started to laugh and the moment was gone.

"Hurry up, you two," called Darryl. "The fire will burn itself out before you get any water on it."

The world's
most gorgeous creep

The next morning I woke up very happy. I lay in bed and thought about Bill and kissing and tennis. I decided I wanted to take lessons right away — in tennis, that is.

Then I remembered that we were going to run away. I knew I was supposed to go to Marna's as soon as possible, but I turned on my stomach and put my head under the pillow. It was so much nicer in bed than it would be listening to Carlie and Steph.

When I did finally get to Marna's, I could see that I should have stayed in bed for the whole day. Steph and Carlie were snarling at each other, and even Marna seemed a little crabby.

"Hi," I said to her. "What's happening?"

"Nice you could finally get here," she snapped back. Marna never snaps at people. I guess Steph and Carlie were really getting to her.

Steph turned to me. "Have you heard Fat Flossie's latest idea? She wants to take a portable TV with her to

47

pass the time."

"But our parents will know we didn't go far if we take a TV," I said.

"Brilliant," said Marna. "Now convince *her.*"

I stared at Marna. She sounded more like Steph than herself. "What's wrong, Marna?" I asked.

Before she had time to answer, Steph started in at Carlie. "You dull bovine, can't you understand anything?"

Carlie turned to us with tears in her eyes. "I'm not going to sit around here and be insulted. Tell me what I'm supposed to bring. I'm going home."

Marna got out a list. "Enough food and clothes for a week. Sleeping bag. Toothbrush. Jane, radio. Carlie, flashlight. Steph, toothpaste and soap. Marna, pots."

"I think I'll bring a hair dryer," said Carlie. "If the TV cameras are there when we come out, we'll want to look good."

"If they want to get all of her in the picture, the camera will have to be too far back to get a good look at her hair," Steph observed to a nearby tree.

I read the letter they'd written to our parents. It said we were safe and would come home when we heard on the six o'clock news that we didn't have to play hockey. I was to slip it under Allison's bedroom door as I left the house.

Steph and Carlie went off together. You could hear them fighting all the way down the street.

"I don't know how those two are going to get through this week without driving each other crazy," I said.

"I'm not worried about them. They like to fight," Marna pointed out. "They must, or they wouldn't hang around together all the time. But I'm afraid I might murder one of them before the week is over."

"Why not both?"

"That's even better."

We laughed, and all of a sudden Marna was herself again. I didn't need to ask what had been the matter: she felt bad about running away. She was worried about Jennie and felt she was deserting her.

I wanted to tell her about my date with Bill, but I didn't know what to say. I knew I couldn't tell her about the last part, unless she asked me about it. I mean, it wasn't the kind of thing you'd just blurt out. Besides, she didn't even ask me if I'd had a good time. I guess she was still jealous. Marna had always liked Bill a little herself.

We talked for a while about our plans, and then I got up to go home. "By the way," Marna said casually, as if she had just thought of it, "there's one thing that has me a little worried."

"What's that?"

"It's something I heard my father say once. For all I know, it's not true . . ." She hesitated.

"What is it, Marna?"

"Well . . . I've heard that when the ice goes out in

the summer and the arena warms up, the whole place gets filled with bats."

"Bats! Oh, no. I hate bats. No, I don't believe it."

We talked it over and decided it was probably just a rumour, but as I walked home I kept thinking about it. Bats really give me the creeps. We had one in our attic once and I was afraid to go upstairs for a long time. Even now I never go to the attic alone.

When I got home Bill was sitting on the front step with two tennis rackets. My arm was still stiff from yesterday, but I didn't complain. We spent the rest of the afternoon hitting balls at the garage door. My mother came out to see what the noise was. When she saw us, she just smiled and went back inside. A little while later she came out and left a pitcher of lemonade on the steps. There are times when she's really not bad to have around.

After dinner, while my parents were watching TV, I got all my stuff together, including some extra clothes and a few books. I got out the letter to our parents and put it in the book I was reading so I wouldn't forget to leave it under Allison's door. I put the book on top of the bundle and hid everything in the closet. Then I went into the kitchen and found some tinned spaghetti, a box of potato chips and some cokes. I also got a couple of mouse traps and some cheese just in case Marna's story about the bats was true. Since they look like mice, I figured maybe they eat like mice.

When I had finished packing, I made a few practice runs on the staircase. The second step from the bottom creaked a bit; I made a note to skip it on the way down. I also found that the screen door squeaked. I put some oil on it, but it didn't help much.

Finally there was nothing left to do but wait. I went into the living room, but my parents barely took their eyes off the television. I sat there and watched them. They looked so comfortable — and unconcerned. I wished I could be there to see their faces when they found out I had disappeared. Maybe then they'd realize that I had a life of my own and wasn't a baby any more.

When the program was over, my father turned to me. "I hear there was a young man over here this afternoon."

Oh no, I thought. Not this routine. I don't know why fathers like this kind of thing so much. "It was only Bill Graydon," I said.

"Only Bill Graydon. *Only,* she says! Marion, did you hear that? Did you ever tell your father it was *only* Hal Tivik?"

My mother frowned at him. "That's enough, Hal. No teasing."

"Since when can't a man tease his own daughter?" Then they started joking back and forth.

When it was time for me to go to bed, I kissed them both good-night. I hadn't done that for a long time, but this was a special occasion. I couldn't go to sleep because if I set the alarm it would wake everyone up when it rang. But I couldn't leave the light on to read either; so I just lay down on the bed and thought about Bill and how I could get him to kiss me again. It helped to pass the time.

Finally it was time to go. I tip-toed to the door and listened. The house was quiet. I picked up my sleeping bag and the food, crept past the door of my parents' room and headed down the stairs. I remembered to skip the creaky step, but I forgot about the screen door. When I opened it, it screeched so loudly I thought it would wake up the whole neighbourhood. I understood why we didn't need a watchdog. I expected to hear my father come pounding down the stairs, but I guess somehow he slept through it.

Sighing with relief, I slipped through the open door and onto the porch. The side lawn was shielded from the street lights by a maple tree. I crossed to the shrubs by the fence. Once I was over that I was on the bicycle path that led to the park beside the arena.

It was very quiet. There is something eerie about being out alone at night when everyone thinks you are safe at home in bed. I was so nervous that I had to give myself a lecture on why there was nothing to worry about. The next thing I knew I was so busy not worrying that I almost blew everything.

There's a jog in the path as it goes past Jamesons'

place. It's there because when everyone else agreed that a bicycle path should be made through the block, old Mr. Jameson refused to give up any of his back yard. He said that the path would become a "haven for illicit activities." It was a long time before I realized he meant that kids would go there to neck. They do, too, but only when they can't get a car.

I was just getting close to Jameson's Jog when I heard voices. At first I thought I was just being jumpy and kept going. Then I heard them again and stopped in my tracks. It was a guy and a girl. They hadn't seen me yet but I was only five or six metres from them.

"It's getting late. I really should be home by now." It was the girl's voice.

"Are you kidding? We just got here."

I peeked around the bend. I couldn't see their faces in the dark, but I didn't need to. I had recognized the voices: it was Jeff Cranley and Janet.

Now I was stuck. There were smooth high fences on both sides of me which I couldn't climb over. If Jeff and Janet came my way, they couldn't help but see me. And if they saw me the whole plan would be ruined. They'd be sure to wonder about my sleeping bag and bundle, and start asking questions. I would have to go back and cut over to the street. But that was too risky, and besides, it would make me late.

I was trying to decide what to do when I heard

Janet's voice again. She sounded scared. "Jeff, please don't. I've really got to go. My parents will wonder . . ."

He laughed. It wasn't a very nice laugh. In fact, if a boy laughed like that when *I* was alone with him in a dark lane, I'd run.

But Janet didn't. Everything was quiet for a minute. Then Jeff spoke. "Make up your mind, Baby," he said. "Every time I turned around you were standing there smiling at me; so I finally asked you out. You liked that, when you could brag to all your friends about who you were going out with, didn't you?"

I didn't hear an answer. He went on. "Well, this is a two-way street, Sweetie. You want to go out with me, you've got to give a little too."

I couldn't believe the guy! I *wouldn't* have if I hadn't heard him myself. Then his voice got soft and cozy. "Don't cry, sweetheart. I just want you to show me that you love me, that's all."

Everything was quiet again.

I haven't had much experience personally, but I do read Ann Landers; so I knew that Jeff's line was not exactly original. And I didn't want Janet to fall for a cornball pitch like that.

I got out my portable radio and turned it on low. Then I started to increase the volume and make some noises so it would sound as if someone was coming. I guess it worked. Janet went running down the path away from me and I heard Jeff swear to himself as he walked off in the same direction.

I turned off the radio, picked up my bundle and set off again, feeling the way St. George must have after he rescued a fair maiden from the dragon. But I guess I would make a lousy knight; the next thing I knew I was staring right into the dragon's face. Jeff had apparently come back to see who had ruined his plans for the evening.

He smiled at me. "Hi, there. Thought I heard someone playing a radio. Are you alone?"

I nodded.

"A sweet young thing like you shouldn't be out by yourself on a night like this," he said.

That was not a new line either. "I'm on my way to my girlfriend's to sleep over," I lied.

"Your parents must be pretty soft to let you out by yourself at this time of night. Want to go somewhere for a coke?"

I couldn't believe my ears. I mean, this was Jeff Cranley! He's a big man around our town — *the* big man, in fact. He goes to all the dances with the best looking girls. He — then I caught myself. I'd just seen this guy in action and here I was still falling for his cornball lines.

"Sorry," I said. "My friend is waiting up for me."

"She'll understand," he said. "You know, I've been watching you for a long time. You're a pretty nice looking chick."

I didn't want to hear any more. I am *not* a nice looking chick — at least no one has ever told me so. I knew I'd better leave fast before I forgot what kind of creep he really was.

"No, thanks," I said. "Good-night."

A look of astonishment spread over his handsome face. I don't think he was used to being turned down by girls. Twice in one night was perhaps some kind of record for him. I never found out if he went on to try for three.

The big break-in

I was late. Marna was at the edge of the ball diamond waiting for me. "What took you so long?" she whispered. "I thought the bats had scared you off."

"I'll tell you later. Where are Steph and Carlie?"

"Waiting by the bushes."

We found them behind the hedge at the back of the arena. "Sorry I'm late," I said. "Is Allison here?"

"She's at the playground with Darryl. I hope she'll be able to tear herself away long enough to do what she's supposed to," said Steph.

"She'll remember," I assured her. "Let's go."

We picked up our stuff and crept to the window of the women's washroom. It was about two metres off the ground and that worried me. We would have to pull ourselves up and through it before the alarm brought Belmer down our necks. I crossed my fingers and hoped he was busy at the other end of town. We would need every second we could get.

Since Steph was the strongest, she was to boost us through and then pull herself in. She knelt down on the ground. I got up on her back and Carlie handed me the flashlight.

"I can see the lock," I whispered. "It's right near the bottom. There's a crack in the frame where I can open it."

"Can you see the alarm wire?"

"Uh-huh. It runs along the glass and through the hinges. Get me a stick."

Carlie found one and handed it to me. I slid it through the crack but the lock wouldn't budge. I pushed on it as hard as I could, praying I wouldn't set off the alarm. Suddenly the lock clicked open. I jumped to the ground.

"Done. As soon as we push the window open, the alarm will go off. Who's first?"

"I'm last," said Steph. "I don't need a boost. Jane, you go first. You can help pull Carlie from the inside. Once she's through, Marna and I will toss in the stuff."

For the next few minutes there was sheer confusion. Steph got down on the ground again, with me on her back. I pushed open the window and the alarm screamed in my ears. Somehow I scrambled in, but as I was helping Carlie she slipped and fell in on me and we landed on the floor in a tangle of arms and legs. We tried to sort ourselves out but by then Steph and Marna were throwing in the sleeping bags and parcels. Marna's head came through next, and finally Steph joined the pile of bodies and junk on the floor.

Marna reached up and closed the window. The noise of the alarm was deafening and she had to shout to be heard. "Where's the flashlight? Good, Carlie. Now, stand still and hold the light on the floor while we get the stuff picked up."

The three of us ran around trying to gather up everything that had fallen out of the bags, but we were so rushed we dropped almost as much as we picked up. I reached for a tin behind Marna and tripped her. She fell into Carlie, who gave a startled yelp and dropped the flashlight. The light went out.

"Now you've done it, you banana," Steph cried. "We'll never find all this stuff in the dark, and Belmer is sure to come in here and see it."

"Shut up, Steph," ordered Marna. "On your hands and knees, everybody. Hurry!"

We crawled around on the concrete floor hunting for tins of tuna and spaghetti. Over the noise of the alarm we didn't hear Belmer's siren, but suddenly there was silence. He was already in the building!

"That's the best we can do," Marna whispered. "Get up on the toilets and don't move."

That part went fairly smoothly, except that Carlie and I both tried to squeeze into the same cubicle. After we'd sorted ourselves out, I got into one of my own and carefully climbed up onto the seat. In about ten seconds my legs started to tremble. I kept wondering how long it would be before I slipped and found myself in a puddle of water. I don't see why public toilets can't have covers like the ones at home.

Then I heard Allison's voice. She was in the arena too. I knew she wouldn't let us down.

"What a rotten trick! Some people just have no respect for the law," she was saying. Her voice oozed sympathy and understanding.

"When we catch them, they'll be sorry," said Constable Belmer angrily. "The inside of a jail cell will teach them that public mischief is no joke."

I didn't like the sound of that at all. My legs shook even more. But Allison's voice just became softer and more sympathetic. "It's really terrible what some people will do. My cousin has told me what a good law-enforcement officer you are. At least most people appreciate what you are doing for Amesbury, even if some don't."

I thought Allison might be laying it on a little thick, but I guess Belmer didn't. He just chuckled as she went on.

"I really am glad you let me see the new arena. It's an interesting building. What are these doors for?"

He started showing her all the rooms off the corridor. "And this is the men's washroom," I heard him say from right next door. "Guess you're not much interested in that."

"No," Allison replied, "but I wonder . . ." Her

voice sank to a whisper.

"Sure, little lady. It's right next door. Just let me check it out first."

My heart leapt into my throat.

"Oh, please," begged Allison, "let me look for you. I've never had a chance to help a real, live detective before."

He fell for it. "Okay. I'll be right outside if you need any help."

The door opened and suddenly the room was flooded with light. I heard each cubicle door open before Allison stepped in beside me. She shut the door behind her and smiled. She stood silent for a few moments, then flushed the toilet.

"Everything okay?" she whispered over the noise of the water.

"Perfect," I answered. I was trying to look dignified, but that's not easy to do when you're crouching on a toilet rim and worried about falling in.

"Well, good luck." She handed me a tin of tuna fish, gave me another quick smile and walked out.

As we were plunged into darkness again, I thought less about my legs and more about Allison. I could hear her going off down the hall chatting away to Belmer, making him feel like a great guy. She had done her part and saved our necks, yet she didn't seem the least bit rattled. She certainly knew how to handle men. I wondered what she would have said to Jeff Cranley if she had met him in a dark alley.

I concentrated again on standing still. A toilet seat is not the easiest place to daydream. I thought I heard the squad car pull out of the parking lot, but no one said a word and no one moved. Suddenly there was a splash from Carlie's cubicle.

I should have been more sympathetic — it could have been me! — but all I could do was giggle. In a moment we were all out on the concrete floor roaring with laughter. Even Carlie joined in, though I noticed she wasn't laughing as hard as the rest of us. I wouldn't have been either, if it had happened to me.

"I'm glad you didn't do that five minutes earlier," gasped Marna. "Can you imagine the look on Belmer's face as he raced in here to rescue you from a watery grave?"

That set us off again. We were feeling so good we decided to have a coke to celebrate. We tried to get the flashlight going, but it wouldn't work. Luckily, Marna had brought a candle. We lit it and sat around eating potato chips and feeling proud of ourselves.

Later we unrolled our sleeping bags and crawled into them. I was so tired I thought I would go right to sleep, but I kept thinking about my mother waking up and finding me gone. She was going to be pretty unhappy.

I noticed a funny sound coming from the sleeping bag beside me. It sounded like a sniffle. Steph sat up. "Someone's blubbering. Carlie?"

"It's not me," Carlie answered in a quivering voice.

"It is so you, you big baby. Stop it right now. It's making me homesick."

"Me too," said Marna.

Soon we were all snivelling — and laughing at the same time, to think we could be such babies. We drew our sleeping bags into a tight circle and put the potato chips in the centre.

I told them about Jeff and Janet. Marna was disgusted with him and Steph was mad, but Carlie said she couldn't understand why I didn't tell him to phone me when I got back. Steph tried to explain it to her, but made the mistake of calling her an imbecile who couldn't balance on the edge of a toilet seat without getting into trouble and that started us all giggling again.

For a while we took turns telling as many jokes as we could remember. I almost fell asleep in the middle of one of Carlie's. It had been going nowhere for ages. Just as I was drifting off I heard Steph ask, "Are you finished yet?"

"No," said Carlie drowsily.

"Well, wake me up when you are. It'll be morning by then."

There was no answer.

"Some joke," muttered Steph. "Ha!"

Exploring
the world of sports

Next morning I woke up to the sound of rushing water. I had been dreaming about standing with Bill beside Niagara Falls, but actually it was just a toilet flushing.

Steph stepped on my hand as she stomped out of the cubicle behind me. "This is ridiculous!" she snapped.

"What?"

"We can't survive under these primitive conditions. There isn't one scrap of toilet paper in the whole place."

I tried to grasp the problem and think of some reply but I wasn't up to it. I turned over, planning to drift off to sleep again, but it was hopeless. My sleeping bag was parked right across the only cubicle anyone wanted to use. There were five other toilets, but for some reason mine was the only one with any appeal.

Carlie was running water and grumbling because she couldn't find any toothpaste and Marna was clawing through the potato chips around my sleeping bag looking for her clothes. Somehow they had disappeared in the night. Then Steph mentioned breakfast and I decided I'd better get up.

She had everything organized. "First we have to find out if the snack bar is open. We need a stove to cook the eggs," she announced.

"Eggs? I wouldn't bother if I were you," said Carlie with a funny smile. "That ride they took through the window last night should have scrambled them already."

Steph looked sick. "I packed them in my clothes to cushion them."

"Don't look now," said Marna; so we all did. The eggs were broken and running all over Steph's blue sweater and clean socks. The day was not starting well at all.

We pushed open the door of the washroom and peered out nervously. The whole arena was lit by two high windows at either end of the rink. But it didn't look like the place we knew. It had always been full of people and noise — the shouts of players, the cheers of spectators, the crack of hockey sticks hitting the puck. Now everything was so quiet we found ourselves whispering as we walked around. The arena seemed enormous and empty and even a little scary.

When we got to the steps that led down to the locker rooms, we walked right by. Suddenly Steph stopped. "Let's go and look," she said.

As far as I know, no girl had ever been down these

stairs, but Steph marched down as if she'd been doing it all her life. There were two doors at the bottom of the staircase. She pushed on the one marked *HOME* and walked in.

"What are we waiting for?" asked Marna as she followed Steph into the locker room.

"Yech," said Carlie when we got inside. "What is that smell?"

"That's sweat," answered Steph. "I get to wash my brother's gym stuff. Imagine what it smells like in here after a busy week!"

"It's awful," said Carlie. "I'm glad I don't ever smell like that."

"How could you?" prodded Steph. "You don't ever move fast enough to get warm. You know, sweating would be a good way for you to lose some of that ugly fat — "

"Shut up, Steph," said Marna.

I looked around. There wasn't much to see. Benches ran along three walls, with hooks above them. I walked into the next room. "Hey, look at the foot baths," I exclaimed.

The girls came rushing in. Steph started to laugh. "You dope. Those are urinals."

"I knew that. I was just fooling," I said quickly. I hadn't the faintest idea what a urinal was.

But Steph wasn't fooled. "They use them to go to the bathroom," she explained.

Carlie looked at her in amazement. "You mean they stand out here in front of everyone and — "

"Of course they do. Honestly, you two don't know very much about boys, do you?"

I tried to change the subject. "I wonder what happened to the shower curtains," I said.

Again Steph burst out laughing. "Boys don't use shower curtains."

I was beginning to feel like a real idiot. "You mean they just take off their clothes and stand there with everybody looking? Naked?"

One reason I've always hated gym is that you have to take off your clothes and stand around in your underwear while you're getting into your gym suit. At the pool in summer all the girls get undressed in the little booths. Don't boys care if other guys see what they look like?

We headed back up the stairs. We still needed to find a place to cook breakfast. The snack bar on the main floor was locked and for a while it looked as if we were going to be eating cold spaghetti for a week, but when we went farther up to the glassed-in lounge where the adults sit to watch the kids play, we found the kitchen unlocked. There was also a washroom with toilet paper, a table, and sofas and easy chairs with loose cushions we could throw on the floor for beds.

After breakfast we moved our things and settled in. Steph washed her sweater and socks and got most of the egg out. I listened to the radio, Carlie slept and Marna wandered off around the arena.

At noon we ate Marna's pie. It was very good, although I wouldn't have chosen lemon meringue for a pie that was going to be thrown through a window. Later we sat on the sofas and turned on my radio for the newscast.

First, we had to sit through all the boring national news. There was one bit about the Egg Marketing Board that sent Carlie into gales of laughter when she looked at Steph.

"And now for the sports," the announcer said.

We looked at each other in dismay. Nothing about us. Weren't we as important as the Prime Minister's latest vacation?

I stopped listening. What had gone wrong? Was my mother so mad at me she didn't even bother to notify the police? Maybe she hadn't realized yet that I was gone. Just then the news announcer broke in with a special bulletin: "Late news flash! The Amesbury Police Department has confirmed reports concerning the disappearance of four teenage girls from their homes last night. There is no reason to suspect foul play. Names will be available on the six o'clock news."

"Well, at least they've noticed we're gone," said Steph.

"Baffled Constables Scour Town!" said Marna. "Runaways Vanish Without a Trace!"

"Belmer may lose some weight," said Carlie. "He won't be able to spend so much time in the café eating doughnuts."

Steph looked at Carlie appraisingly. "Speaking of fat people eating, what is that you're putting in your mouth?"

We all looked at Carlie. She was sprawled on the sofa within easy reach of a dish of peanuts. She looked back at us guiltily. "Get off my back, Steph."

"I'm only saying this for your own good — but don't you really think you're just a little bit tubby?"

"No," said Carlie. "I just have heavy bones, so I look bigger than the rest of you."

"Get off it, Carlie. You know you'd love to be thin like Marna."

Everyone looked at Marna next. I picked up one of Carlie's movie magazines and started flipping the pages. I had a horrible feeling my turn might be coming and I wanted to avoid it if I could.

"Well, I'm no fatter than Jane," Carlie said.

I could have strangled her. Carlie is fat; I'm just a little plump. When everyone looked my way, I just kept reading. At least, I kept turning the pages.

"Yes, Jane's pretty bad too," said Steph.

I pretended I didn't hear.

"In a minute, we won't be speaking to one another," Marna warned. "And if we don't get out of this room and do something, we'll all just lie around eating peanuts. How about a game?"

Carlie and I looked at Marna in amazement. Games are for phys. ed. periods — I hate them. "Not for me, thanks," I said. "I want to start my book."

"Me neither," said Carlie. "I'm napping. Steph's snoring kept me awake all night."

"Never mind them, Marna," said Steph. "Let sleeping cows lie. Let's go down and find something to do."

When they were gone I looked at the pictures in another magazine and Carlie settled onto the sofa. Everything was peaceful.

"Those two make me sick," said Carlie. "They think that just because they weigh less than we do they're better than we are."

I didn't want to get involved in that conversation. I was still mad at Carlie for saying I was as fat as she was. I kept reading and soon she got tired of trying to talk to me. She lay on the sofa for a while and stared at the ceiling. Then she started talking to herself.

"Steph hates me. Marna never says a word to me. Jane lies there and reads a magazine right in my face. Fat people aren't jolly. They're the loneliest people in the world." When Carlie starts feeling sorry for herself, she really does a job.

I put down my magazine. "Carlie, stop that. I don't hate you; I just want to read. Steph and Marna both asked you to go and do whatever they're doing. You're the one who said you wouldn't."

Carlie thought that over, never taking her eyes from the ceiling. Suddenly a shriek of laughter came up from the rink. Carlie got up and walked to the door. "They sure are making a lot of noise. I'll go down and tell them to keep it quiet. We don't want everyone to know we're here."

She left and I thought about starting my book, but I couldn't concentrate. Carlie's voice had joined in the screams and shouts coming from the rink. I got up to look.

The three of them were running around on the boards that cover the floor of the rink when the ice is out. They each had a broken hockey stick and they were chasing a rubber ball. Two rubber boots at one end formed the only goal. No matter who got the ball, the other two turned on her and tried to get it away. They were all bumping into each other, laughing and shouting.

I put down my magazine. "You wait right here," I said. "I'll be back." Talking to yourself must be contagious.

Attack and TATTLE

When I got down to the rink, I hung around for a while beside the boards. Soon there was a break in the action and Marna noticed me. "Good, Jane. I knew you'd get here sooner or later. Come and play. We call it *Attack!*"

"Oh, I don't think so, Marna. I'd rather just watch."

"That's what I said," Carlie shrieked from the other side of the rink. "Come on, Jane. I just got a goal."

"Stop shouting. Someone will hear you."

"Not a chance," said Steph. "When this arena is full of fans you can hardly hear them outside. No one would be able to hear four voices even if we screamed at the top of our lungs. Here's a stick."

I shook my head and they started playing again. It was pretty easy to score. The goal was about three metres wide and there was no goalie. The best way to keep anyone from scoring was to shoot the ball down to the far end of the rink. By the time someone else had brought it back, she was too tired to move very fast.

Then you could rush in, take the ball away and score yourself.

I watched Carlie chugging up and down the ice for a while and realized that she didn't have the slightest idea how to handle Marna and Steph. They could run fast, but I knew I could show them a thing or two.

Grabbing up the stick they'd left for me, I rushed into the game just as Steph was running down the rink. She didn't see me coming until I was right in front of her. I think it scared her to see someone charging in from nowhere. She drew back and I grabbed the ball. One swing and it was sailing down the ice and right into the goal.

"Cheater," Steph screamed. "No fair!"

"What was unfair about that?" I yelled back. "One for me. What's the score?"

When I found out it was thirty-two for Steph, twenty-eight for Marna and fourteen for Carlie, I wasn't quite so happy. But they agreed to start a new game now that we were all there, and all afternoon we thumped and bumped around the arena. When the dust cleared, Steph had seventy-three goals, Marna had sixty-eight, Carlie and I were almost tied in last place with forty-nine and forty-seven.

The game was fun until Carlie hurt her hand. She claimed that the pain was too severe for her to hold a stick, but I think she just couldn't move another step. I was just as happy, because I couldn't either.

We were all so dirty that we limped down to the locker room for a shower. The hot water felt so great on my sore body that I wanted to stay in the shower forever — and I never even thought about there being no curtains. Afterwards we sat around in our towels and discussed the rules of the game.

Suddenly Carlie exclaimed, "What would the Arlies say if they could see us now?"

We looked at each other. Four girls sitting in the locker room was certainly a first for Amesbury.

"That's easy," said Steph. "They'd say, 'Get those naked women out of our change room!' "

"They certainly would notice us," I agreed.

"It's one way of being a pioneer," said Marna.

"The best way," Steph pointed out. "They didn't have showers in covered wagons."

For some reason Steph's remark struck us as funny. While we dressed we joked about taking a wagon train across the prairies and drawing our wagons into a circle and cooking pemmican for dinner. We even decided that pemmican might be an improvement on pork and beans, but that didn't keep us from emptying a couple of cans when we went back upstairs.

At six o'clock we turned on the radio just in time, because we were the very first item. The newscaster gave our names and addresses and said anyone knowing our whereabouts should call the police. Then he went on:

"Interviews with the parents seem to indicate that the girls have run away in an attempt to draw public attention to the fact that, because of their sex, they are not being allowed to participate in the town's organized hockey program.

"Mrs. Klee, mother of one of the runaways, says she hopes this protest will make the town aware of the unfairness of this discriminatory rule to half the population — "

"What?" Carlie exploded. "How could she!"

"Shh!"

" — interviews with the other parents which seem to confirm this story. The girls sent in their applications, but were told that they would not be permitted to play.

"Do you think that girls have a place on the hockey rinks of this nation? Tomorrow night at six, hear comments by two concerned adults on Citizen's Corner, and then voice your own opinions on the Amesbury Hot-Line.

"And now for the national news . . . "

"What's going on here?" said Steph. "Did you all hear what I heard?"

"How could they do this to us?" asked Marna. "There must be some mistake. My mother wouldn't lie for no reason."

"What do you mean, no reason? There are lots of reasons." Carlie sounded furious. "We had them beat the moment we ran away. They knew they'd have to give in. It's my mother. I should have known."

"What on earth are you talking about?" asked Marna.

"I know exactly what happened," said Carlie. "I know my mother. She wakes up this morning and finds I'm not there. She calls Jane's mother and when they find the note we left — "

Suddenly I felt rather sick.

Carlie continued, " — right away her brain starts working. She suggests that they ignore the note and pretend we ran away to force the association to let us play hockey. So she gets all your mothers together for coffee."

"Carlie — " I tried to interrupt but no one paid any attention. They were all too busy listening to Carlie's story unfold. She was really laying it on.

" 'We want our daughters back,' they insist. 'I want that too,' my mother agrees, 'but don't forget there is a principle at stake here.' She talks to them for a while and convinces them that this principle is worth any sacrifice, even if it means betraying their own daughters!"

"Carlie — " I tried again, but it was no use. No one even turned to look at me. I got up and walked to my bag of books.

"So they destroy the letter and claim that we told them we *want* to play hockey. The truth is all too plain: our mothers have betrayed us!"

I walked back to the group and held out my hand. "I think you'd better look at this," I said quietly.

But Carlie was in a fever pitch of anger. "Let's face the facts. They've sold us down the river! They've thrown us to the sharks! They've — "

"Look at me!" I yelled.

All three heads swivelled around.

"You're wrong, Carlie. Here's our letter. I forgot to leave it for Allison."

All three mouths fell open. Steph got up and looked at me.

"I had it right in this book so I wouldn't forget . . ." My voice trailed off. There really didn't seem to be much I could say.

No one else said anything either. They just looked at me. I went to a sofa and sat down with my back to them. I don't think I've ever felt worse in my life. I had ruined everything. My eyes felt itchy. I shut them to keep from crying.

Then Marna came over and put her arm around me. It felt just like my mother and I opened my eyes, almost hoping the whole thing had been a horrible dream. "Anyone can make a mistake, Jane. Don't worry. We'll think of a way to straighten things out." I don't think I've ever liked anyone better than I liked Marna right then.

We sat there, no one saying anything. Suddenly Marna asked, "Did you hear that?"

"I didn't hear a thing," said Steph.

"Shh!"

We were all still. We could hear a faint ringing sound.

"It's the pay phone in the lobby."

We rushed out of the lounge and down the stairs. The phone was ringing like crazy. We looked at each other.

"Must be a wrong number," said Carlie.

At that moment the ringing stopped.

"Guess you're right," said Steph.

Then it started again.

"Maybe it's Allison," I thought out loud. "She said she would try to get the number here so she could call us."

"But how could she? Pay phones aren't listed in the phone books."

It kept ringing.

"Answer it, Jane," said Steph. "Pretend you're the operator. Ask what number they're calling. If it's not Allison, hang up quick."

I picked up the ringing phone and took a deep breath.

"What number are you calling, please?" I asked in my most nasal voice.

"Hi, Jane," Allison said. "What took you so long? Having a bath?"

"Allison!" I almost shouted. All the girls looked relieved. "How did you get the number?"

"I memorized it during Belmer's tour. How are you all doing?"

"Terrible," I said. "Didn't you hear the news?"

"Yes! Where's that letter? I looked everywhere for it."

"It's right here with me. I forgot to leave it."

"Oh, brother," Allison groaned. "Now what are you going to do?"

"I don't know. Have you got any ideas?"

"I guess you can't get out and mail the letter — or pass it out to me?"

"Not without setting off the alarm."

"What about calling the radio station? Just to give your side of the story."

"Hey, Allison, good idea! That just might work. We'll talk about it."

"Here's some news that might cheer you up. You had two phone calls today. Bill wanted to know if you were all right. I said you were fine. And the guy who was at the lake called. I guess he doesn't listen to the news. He didn't know you had left home."

"You mean Jeff Cranley?" I asked in amazement.

"The one and only. He said he'd call back."

"I really don't think I care," I said, trying to sound sophisticated.

"Good. I'll tell him the next time he calls." She sounded pleased at the thought.

When I hung up, I told the girls about Allison's idea of calling the radio station.

"Great," said Steph. "Let's do it now. Who's got some change?"

We went through our pockets. I had a five dollar bill, Steph and Marna had some ones, and Carlie didn't have a cent.

"We could go through the operator," suggested Carlie.

"But we'd have to give the number here, wouldn't we? And then she'd know where we were."

"One more good idea down the drain," said Carlie, glaring at me.

I tried to change the subject. "Jeff Cranley called me."

"Are you bragging or complaining?" asked Steph.

"I guess I'm complaining. Every time I think of him with poor Janet I could scream. I think he's a real — "

"A real what?" asked Carlie.

"I don't know. I can't think of a rotten enough word."

"How about creep?"

"No, that isn't specific enough."

"Jerk? Goof? Dolt?"

Somehow nothing seemed quite right, but we kept trying. When we ran out of ideas we looked through the dictionary Marna had brought with her Scrabble game, and finally we found the right word: *lecher, a man immoderately given to sexual indulgence.* That sounded a lot like Jeff Cranley.

"I know," said Steph. "We should start a Lecher List. Anyone who finds out a guy is the Jeff Cranley type can report him, and we'll put his name on the list. That way he won't be able to get any dates."

"Great idea," said Carlie. "But how do we get the names? Guys aren't exactly pounding down my front door for a chance to lech *me.*"

It was a good point. None of us had guys begging to take us into dark laneways.

"That doesn't matter," said Steph. "All we need is some help from girls like Sandra Stephans."

"But why would she want to help us?" I asked.

"Because it would help her to compare notes with other girls. If we all pooled our information, everyone would be better off. I even have a name for the organization," Steph mused. "We could call it 'The Association To Trap Lechers Early.' "

"Won't that be sort of hard to remember?" I asked.

"Not when you see what the first letters spell," said Steph.

We thought for a minute — then grinned. And that's how TATTLE was born.

The
midnight pizza party

There were no potato chips and cokes in bed that night. We had eaten everything you could possibly consider a snack. All that was left were things like pork and beans, which no one even wanted for dinner, let alone in bed after the lights were out. But at least the sleeping arrangements were a little nicer than they had been the night before. A washroom floor is not my idea of first class accommodation.

We didn't think we should put lights on in case someone might see them from the park; so we went to bed early. I was happy to crawl into my sleeping bag and snuggle down into the sofa cushions. We had played another game of Attack after supper and muscles I hadn't even known about were screaming at me in pain.

We talked for a long time about TATTLE, and had fun trying to agree on boys who were probable candidates for our Lecher List.

Steph thought we should start up a monthly newsletter with a list of boys to ignore and places to avoid. Carlie suggested we ask Allison to be our foreign correspondent and to answer letters and give advice until we got enough experience to do the column ourselves. I fell asleep before we had decided on a name for the paper, but I was sure they would call it *The Tattler.* I didn't see the point in waiting around.

The next thing I knew, I was sitting bolt upright in bed, sure that the house was on fire. Bells were ringing like crazy.

"Jane!" shouted Marna. "Wake up! Get moving! Someone's set off the alarm. Belmer will be here any minute. Carlie, get up!"

Steph and Marna were rushing around grabbing things and shoving them into the little washroom off the lounge. I scurried out of my sleeping bag and tried to get it hidden under the nearest sofa. Then I grabbed the cushions I had been sleeping on and put them back in place. It was so dark that we kept bumping into each other.

Then the alarm stopped ringing. Belmer was in the building! I groped my way into the washroom, but as soon as I got there I knew something was wrong. It took me a moment to figure out what — there were only three of us there!

"Where's Carlie?" I asked.

Steph muttered something, then opened the door and stuck her head out into the lounge. "Carlie," she whispered. "Where are you? Get in here. He's coming!"

"Okay, Mother, I'll be right there," Carlie answered. "I'm almost dressed."

"I thought her sleeping bag was awfully heavy," Marna giggled. "I rolled her under the couch."

Carlie had slept through the whole thing!

"We've still got time," Steph urged. "Grab a corner and we'll get her in here."

We ran out and got hold of the bag. "I'm coming," Carlie murmured as we dragged her across the floor.

Then the lights went on. From the look on Belmer's face, I'd say he was even more surprised than we were. "Good Heavens!" he exclaimed. "What are you doing?"

"Hiding the body," Steph snapped.

He looked at us nervously. Then he walked over and took a long look at Carlie. She rolled over and buried her head under the top flap of the sleeping bag.

With a relieved look on his face, he turned and looked at the rest of us. "So this is where you've been hiding," he said. "How did you get in here?"

No one answered. After glaring at us for a moment, he managed to figure it out. "Last night? With some help from a nice young girl from Chicago?"

We nodded.

"I think you'd all better sit down for a minute or two while I think this over."

We lined up on the sofa across from him. He stood there staring down at us as if he still couldn't believe what he'd found. As we waited, I looked around. Even if we'd managed to hide Carlie, Belmer would have known we were there. Steph's clothesline was still up, and except for the stuff that was thrown on the floor, it held every piece of clothing we had brought. There were lots of dirty dishes all over the counter, and our broken hockey sticks were lying on the floor.

Finally Constable Belmer sat down too. "I'd better get on the phone right away," he said half-heartedly. "Your parents are very worried. And I'll have to get you down to the station. Breaking and entering, it will be. That's a very serious charge. Pack your things, girls. I'll go and call in."

He stood up and started slowly towards the door. I couldn't understand what was wrong. He had caught us red-handed. He would be a big hero, and yet he didn't seem very happy about it.

"There's just one thing, Constable Belmer," Steph said suddenly. "What do you think people will say when they find out that you checked out the arena the night we ran away? I mean, four life-size girls might seem a bit difficult to miss."

He came back and sat down again, with a huge sigh. "I know exactly what they'll say," he muttered. "They already think I'm too old for this job. They'll say they should get someone who understands kids better than I do. This is just the kind of excuse they're looking for to force me to retire."

That made me feel bad. Belmer is not a great cop, but he isn't a bad guy. He's not at all like the cops you see on TV, and not the type who could ever break up an international drug ring, but then I can't imagine an international drug ring operating out of Amesbury anyway.

"I think you understand kids fine," said Marna quietly. She really is a very kind person.

He smiled up at her. "Thank you. But I don't think that will help much when they find out about this."

"Of course," Steph began again, "it would look a whole lot better if we were to turn up somewhere else. What if we gave ourselves up outside? Then it wouldn't be your fault at all."

"But he found us here," said Marna.

"I don't see what difference it makes to us where he finds us," I said bitterly. "We're still found."

"But if we agreed to help him, then he could help us a bit too," said Steph. "What do you say to that, Constable Belmer?"

We looked at him. He obviously hadn't heard the question. "That's right," he mused. "Then they couldn't say a thing . . . " He brightened. "Hurry and gather your things, girls. I can say you turned up in the park."

"Not so fast," said Steph. "If we agree to give ourselves up, couldn't you agree to let us stay for just one more day?"

"Absolutely not," he said emphatically. "Your parents are too worried."

"But we're safe here," Marna argued. "Where could we be safer? And if we did get into any trouble, we could just ring the alarm, and you'd be here to look after us."

"Besides, if you take us home now, we'll have to run away again. And next time we'll have to hitch-hike out of town," added Steph.

"You wouldn't! That's crazy! You could really get into bad trouble — "

"Exactly. Come on, this is your chance to show how well you understand kids. We just want one more day."

"Let me think about it," said Belmer. "Sounds like blackmail to me." He thought for a moment. "If I do agree, do you promise never to run away again?"

We all promised.

"What about her?" he asked, pointing to the lump in Carlie's sleeping bag.

"Does she look like a troublemaker?" asked Steph.

"Okay, but you'll have to tell me exactly what you're up to before I make up my mind." He settled back comfortably in his chair, clasping his hands behind his head. "By the way, did you hear about the duck who went into the restaurant and ordered a bowl of soup and quackers?"

We looked at each other and grinned. Same old

Belmer, same old joke.

We started to tell him about the mess we were in, but before we got anywhere he asked if we by any chance had a doughnut. "I was on my way for a coffee break when the alarm went off," he explained.

Marna laughed. "Doughnuts? Are you kidding? The best we could offer you is a can of pork and beans."

"Don't you have anything else?" he asked.

"Tinned spaghetti," offered Steph.

He groaned. "You four wait right here," he said, and left the room.

We waited. Then we heard a car in the parking lot. Steph went to the window and peered through the curtains.

"He's going," she said. "I guess he'll be back after he gets his doughnut."

We sat down to wait for him, but that got boring pretty quickly. We put our beds back together and got all the stuff out of the washroom. Then we dragged Carlie back to the middle of the room. Since Belmer hadn't come back, we got into bed and lay there waiting.

I was just dozing off when I heard the door to the arena open. "He's back," I said. "At least I hope it's him."

When he walked through the door, I couldn't believe my nose. He was carrying a large pizza and a carton of soft drinks. He grinned as we all crowded around him.

"Couldn't let the hockey team die of malnutrition," he said.

"I'll get the plates," offered Marna.

"Look at the pepperoni," crowed Steph.

Suddenly Carlie woke up. "Who — what's going on? I was having a great dream — about pizza. I can still smell it — " She stopped. She had seen Belmer.

"A man!" she shrieked. "A man in my bedroom! Help!" She tried to run out of the room in her sleeping bag, but it didn't work.

Constable Belmer walked over and shook her arm. "Relax, Carlie. It's me, Constable Belmer. I've come to help you. I brought you a pizza. Here, have some."

He didn't need to say another word. Carlie kicked her way out of the sleeping bag and went to work on the pizza. After a few minutes of concentrated eating, she looked at him curiously. "What are you doing here?"

He explained about the alarm going off.

"I don't believe it," said Carlie. "We would have heard it."

"We did hear it," Marna assured her. "You were the only one who slept through it all."

"I'm a very sound sleeper," said Carlie proudly. "My mother has to call me for hours before I hear her in the morning."

"Funny how the smell of pizza managed to wake you up," said Steph. "Maybe your mother should just pass a slice of bacon under your nose each morning."

"Not a bad idea. Can I go back to bed now?"

"Why not?" grumbled Steph. "You've eaten all the pizza."

She had, too. We'd been so busy watching her we hadn't noticed that she got three pieces while we had only one.

"It's late," said Belmer. "You girls should all be in bed."

"But what have you decided?" asked Marna.

"I'm going to leave you here till tomorrow night. Then I'm coming to get you. Even if they don't say you can play hockey, you'll have to go home."

"But we don't want to play!" shouted Carlie from the depths of her sleeping bag.

"Then why did you run away?" he asked, confused.

As we got into our sleeping bags, we explained the whole situation. I told him about the letter I had forgotten to leave for Allison.

"But you still haven't explained why you don't want to play hockey," he said.

"How would you like to be the only man in a ballet school?" Steph asked.

Belmer looked down at his bulging stomach. "I think that might be tutu much," he said.

We all giggled.

He stood there watching us, his hand on the light switch. "Good night, girls. I'll see you tomorrow."

For a horrible moment I thought he was going to tuck

us all in. He sounded just like a parent.

"Take care," he said, and switched off the light.

We heard his footsteps echoing down the stairs. I closed my eyes and lay there feeling very safe in the big dark room.

Dirty tricks

When I woke up next morning, I thought Belmer had put poison in the pizza. My calf and arm muscles were paralysed. Steph grinned as she watched me sit up.

"Feeling a little stiff? Me too. I think someone spent the night beating me with a hockey stick. I guess Attack was a little hard on our poor, frail bodies."

We didn't eat much breakfast. After a quick tuna sandwich, we sat down to think about what we should do.

"We have to make a decision by tonight," Steph said. "Belmer won't leave us here any longer than that."

"We could always run away again," suggested Carlie.

"We promised we wouldn't," Marna reminded her.

"*You* promised you wouldn't. I was asleep at the time. I don't have to go along with any promises made for me while I was asleep."

"Fine, Carlie," I said. "If you want to run away by yourself, go ahead, but none of us will go with you."

Her face fell. "I can't go by myself."

"Right," said Steph. "Now, what are we going to do when we get out of here? And what do we do about the fact that the whole town now thinks we want to play hockey, thanks to Jane here? Even if the hockey association decides we can't, everyone will still think we're dying to."

"And our mothers think we agreed with them," added Marna. "They'll never believe us now when we go back and tell them what really happened."

"So we have the choice of trying to explain things and looking dumb, or leaving them the way they are and looking dumber," finished Steph.

No one seemed to have anything more to add. I certainly didn't — I'd done enough damage as it was. As soon as I could, I got up and went for a walk around the arena to get away from everyone. I didn't want to think things out — that was too depressing. I just wanted to be alone.

I sat down in the dimly lit stands and stared down at the rink. I could imagine Bill skating down the ice, blasting in a hard shot, and me leaning over the boards cheering like mad when he scored. But somehow I just couldn't imagine the whole situation the other way round.

"Jane!"

It was Marna. The girls were getting ready to play again. I didn't answer.

"Maybe she's hiding so she doesn't have to play," said Carlie.

The three of them appeared on the rink and started without me. I tried not to pay attention, but I knew that I could do a better job than Carlie at blocking Steph's shots. I got my stick.

We played for an hour, and towards the end things got pretty bitter. I know now why fights break out in the middle of games — when you work that hard, you really start to care. That's how Marna got the bloody nose. I didn't mean to hit her with my stick, but I sure did want to get that goal. I tried to apologize, but Marna yelled at me for being so clumsy, and that made me so mad that I almost hit her again.

After an unusually quiet lunch, we rested. I read my book, Marna and Steph played Scrabble and Carlie looked through a movie magazine. She kept interrupting to tell us who had what painted on the bottom of his swimming pool, and how many stereo speakers someone else had in her house. Since none of us expressed much interest, she eventually switched to a fashion and beauty guide. It had a good section on hairdos. Carlie tore out the pages and showed us the drawings of different styles. You could cut them out and try them on your face to see what you'd look like in different haircuts.

She dragged us all into the little washroom off the lounge and stood us in front of the mirror to try them. Marna didn't look bad in long black hair with bangs, and Steph looked hilarious in one of those frizzy styles. I looked terrible in all of them.

"Hey, Carlie, that looks great!" said Steph.

I turned to look. She was right. Carlie had tried on a short blonde cut and it looked an awful lot better than the long straggly hair that was always getting in her face.

"I like it too," said Marna. "You should think about getting your hair cut, Carlie."

"Don't think about it. Let's do it," urged Steph.

"No," Carlie refused flatly. "My mother is always saying the same thing. She hates my hair. But it's my hair and I'm going to keep it."

"You must be crazy, Carlie. Look in the mirror," ordered Steph.

We all looked again. The short hair really did make a difference. Her face didn't look so fat, and she didn't seem as messy as she usually did.

"I like it, Carlie," I said.

"So do I," she answered. "But I've fought with my mother for so long about it that I hate to give in. I'll have to think about it." She folded the drawing up and put it in her jeans pocket. "Want to try on some make-up?" she asked, to change the subject. "I brought all kinds of stuff along."

"Sure," said Marna.

Carlie left the washroom to get her things. When she had gone Steph turned to us. "She's so stubborn. She never wants to do what's good for her."

"Leave her alone, Steph," said Marna. "It's her hair, not yours."

Steph didn't answer.

Carlie came back with an enormous make-up bag. In it she had nail polish, lipsticks, blush-on, eye shadow and even false eyelashes.

"Where did you get all this?" I asked. I own one tube of lipstick and some foundation to cover pimples.

"I bought it," she said. "I like to try it out. I'm not very good yet, though. It takes a lot of practice."

"I want to try the eyelashes," said Marna.

"Here, I'll help," I said.

She had apparently forgiven me for hitting her in the nose. We started putting eye shadow on each other. It's not as easy as you'd think. It went onto my fingers beautifully, but it didn't seem to want to come off onto Marna's eyelids.

Carlie was watching us and laughing. "I'm not very good yet, but I'm better than you," she said. "Here, let me try."

Steph, who was standing right beside her, said, "Carlie, about that haircut . . . "

"No, Steph. I don't want — "

Steph held up her hands. In one she had the scissors Carlie had used to cut out the hairdos; in the other, a long piece of Carlie's hair.

"That's a rotten trick, Steph," said Marna.

"Nonsense. She'll like it once it's short. Won't you, Carlie?"

Carlie glared. "I don't see what choice I have now. But you'd better do a good job!"

"Don't worry. I've cut lots of hair before. Besides, it tells you how to do it right in the magazine."

Steph opened the book and started to pin Carlie's hair up on top of her head. She really looked as if she knew what she was doing. She sat Carlie up on the sink with her back to the mirror and went to work.

While Steph was cutting, Marna and I went back to fixing our eyes, with Carlie giving instructions. Pretty soon I had the eyelashes on Marna — and hardly any glue at all on her face.

When Marna opened her eyes, the eyelashes looked beautiful, but she didn't even go and look at herself. She just stared at Carlie. "Steph," she said in a strangled voice, "don't you think that's short enough?"

I turned — and gasped. Carlie looked almost bald! Maybe it was because her hair was pretty well the same colour as her skin, or maybe we were just used to seeing her with lots of hair, but she looked awful.

Carlie must have realized from the look on our faces that something had gone wrong. She brushed away Steph's hand, stood up and slowly turned to look in the mirror.

"It'll look better when I'm finished," Steph said apologetically.

It couldn't have looked worse. In some places it was no more than a couple of centimetres long; in others, three times that. The bangs sloped rakishly up across her forehead and one ear looked higher than the other.

Carlie just stood there and stared. Finally she turned to Steph.

"Sorry," said Steph weakly. "I didn't mean — "

"Please leave, all of you. I would like to be alone."

Carlie's calmness scared me more than anything else she could have said or done. I couldn't remember her ever being too mad at Steph to shout or cry, but that time she was. One by one, we filed past her and out to the lounge.

"That was rotten, Steph," said Marna. "How could you?"

"I didn't do it on purpose. I was trying to follow the directions, but one side got too short. When I tried to fix it, the other side got even shorter. Do you think I *want* her to look that freaky? I'm the one who has to walk down the street with her."

"I don't think you need to worry about that. I doubt that she'll ever speak to you again."

"If I were you, I would hide all the knives," I suggested, "just in case she decides to stab you in the middle of the night."

The door to the washroom opened. Slowly, with dignity, Carlie emerged.

Steph went over to her. "Carlie — "

Carlie raised her hand. "I don't want to discuss it. I'm sure it was an accident. We'll just forget it."

I couldn't believe my ears. Neither could Steph, I'm sure, but Carlie seemed to mean it. For the rest of the afternoon she sat and read magazines as if nothing had happened. I went back to my book and Steph and Marna finished their Scrabble game.

When Steph got up to go to the bathroom, Carlie jumped up too. "Sorry, Steph. I'm in a bit of a rush. Can I go first?"

"Sure." That afternoon Steph would have agreed to anything Carlie asked.

When Carlie had closed the door behind her, Steph turned to us. "Has she really forgiven me? That's not like her at all."

"If she has, it's more than you deserve," answered Marna.

Carlie came back out. "The light bulb has burned out in there, and someone left the top off my nail polish. I knocked it over."

We could smell it.

"Sorry, Carlie," I said. "It must have been me. I thought I put the top back on."

"This sure isn't my day," she said. "Oh well, never mind. Your turn, Steph." She sat down and picked up her magazine.

Steph went into the washroom. The moment she closed the door, Carlie got back up and walked over to it. For the first time since she had seen herself in the mirror, she was smiling.

Marna looked at her. "What's going on, Carlie?"

Carlie put her finger to her lips and motioned for us to come over to the door. She pushed it open a crack and we peeked in. I couldn't see anything in the dark, but I heard Steph tear off some toilet paper. Then I guess she tried to stand up.

"What the — ouch!" she yelled. There was a thud. Her head must have cracked into the door. "Carlie. Get in here!"

"Don't yell, Steph. I'm right here," Carlie answered pleasantly, opening the door.

"What did you put all over the toilet seat? It's sticky."

"Just a little glue," said Carlie. "Eyelash glue. Safe for all skin."

She was grinning. So were we.

"Very funny, Carlie. Good joke. But did you really think I'd get stuck? Eyelash glue could hardly be strong enough to keep fifty kilograms of person on a toilet seat."

"I didn't want to stick you there forever, Steph. Come on out and we'll get it off."

"But I can't pull up my pants. They'll get stuck."

"Well, then, wait until it dries. I'll fix the light."

Carlie was grinning even more. Poor old Steph was caught with her pants down, as the expression goes. I was kind of sorry she hadn't stuck. It would have served her right.

"I'm dry," she said at last, stepping out of the cubicle.

Carlie was kneeling on the counter screwing the light bulb tight. Steph looked up at her. "Well, I guess we're even," she said. "I know I deserved it. You sure scared me."

"I think you got off easy," said Marna. "Carlie still has to live with her hair."

"Steph's not finished yet," said Carlie slowly. " I just put the glue on so she would give herself time to dry."

"Why?" asked Steph.

Carlie turned to us. "I think we should leave. Steph will want to be alone to have the first view of herself. Look behind you, Steph."

Obediently, we went out the door, not sure what was going on. Steph must have stood up on the counter to get a look at herself in the mirror. All of a sudden she let out a terrific shout.

"Carlie, what have you done?" Marna asked.

"Added three bottles of nail polish to the glue and poured all the nail polish remover down the sink," Carlie explained happily.

Marna opened the door. There for all to see was a sight I'll never forget. A bright red ring encircled Steph's pure white behind.

* * *

We tried to get it off, but nothing seems to remove nail polish as well as nail polish remover does, and that was all down the drain. Of course, the glue made things even worse.

But the fight was over. It's very difficult to stay mad while scraping nail polish off a person's behind. Carlie was laughing so hard that she couldn't keep on sulking.

"I didn't think you had it in you," said Steph.

"Thank you," Carlie said modestly. "It just came to me."

"But I didn't mean to wreck your hair."

"What difference does that make? You had no business cutting it in the first place. You always think you know what's best for me."

"Okay, so I nag you. But it's for your own good."

"I think it's for *your* own good," Carlie countered. "You don't really want me for a friend. If you did, you'd quit trying to change me."

"But I do. You're my best friend."

"Then how come you're always trying to make me into someone I'm not?"

All of a sudden Carlie didn't seem as dumb as we thought she was. Marna and I decided to leave her alone with Steph, since their conversation seemed private. Besides, it gave me a chance to get a few things off my own chest.

"I'm sorry about hitting you this morning," I said. "I didn't know you'd get so mad."

"It wasn't that so much," Marna answered. "I guess I was still upset about Saturday."

"Saturday? What about it?"

"You don't even remember. Saturday you were supposed to come over to my house. We were going to go shopping."

"But, Marna, I had a date! We can shop anytime."

"I'm just as important as Bill Graydon, aren't I?"

"Well sure, but . . ."

"Do you mean we can't ever plan anything anymore, just in case some boy asks you out?"

I didn't know what to say. I didn't know how to tell her I'd drop *anything* for Bill, even just to go and watch him wash his car. After all, he's really special. But then, so is Marna. She's my best friend and we've spent our whole lives together. I couldn't imagine what it would be like without her around whenever I wanted her.

"I'm sorry," I said. "I didn't mean — "

"Careful," warned Marna. "Don't apologize if you don't mean it. But think how you'd feel if you were me."

I thought about it for a minute. "I really am sorry," I said.

The great debate

That evening at six o'clock we gathered around the radio again. The news was all bad, as usual. In fact it was so depressing that I decided never to listen to it again. Then the sports went on for ages. Since I don't keep track of which team is which, I couldn't tell if it was good news or bad. Baseball was big, but there was lots of football news and even some for hockey — which is pretty surprising since it was still the middle of the summer. How do guys have room in their heads for all that stuff? No wonder girls do better in school than boys do. They don't have all those teams and scores to remember. Finally the news was over.

After a few commercials, the announcer's voice came on again. "Now it's time for Citizen's Corner. Here's a chance for the people of Amesbury to voice their opinions on today's question: Do girls have a place on the hockey rinks of Canada? First, allow me to present the chairman of the Amesbury Hockey Association, Mr. Hal Tivik."

My father hates speaking in public. He isn't very good at it and it makes him very nervous. I guess that's why he spent his whole time presenting facts. He believes in facts. He thinks that if people understand the facts they will always reach the right conclusion — *his* conclusion.

So he announced how many boys played hockey in Amesbury every year, how many went on to play in higher leagues, and how many hours of ice time were already scheduled. Then he estimated the number of girls who might want to play and showed how impossible it would be to find ice time for them. It was obvious that he had done his homework, but he was incredibly dull. When he was finished, I felt I could never agree with anyone that boring, whether he was right or not.

Then it was Mrs. Klee's turn. You had to hand it to her — she was far from dull. She didn't sound nervous either. She just took the mike and let loose.

"The town of Amesbury has always been very proud of its tradition of fine athletes. It has produced many stars for our great national sport. It has . . ." She went on listing all the reasons why our hockey program was so great. Anyone who didn't know her would have wondered which side she was on. She's pretty sneaky.

Then she got a little louder. "I have a teenage daughter I'm very proud of."

Carlie tried to look modest.

"One day not long ago we were having one of our heart-to-heart talks and we began discussing the fact that the enjoyment of the wonderful sport of hockey is completely denied to the young girls of Amesbury. Together we shared our anguish over that fact. Then and there I assured my daughter that the situation would be remedied."

"Lies. All lies, Mother," said Carlie.

"Shortly afterwards we submitted her application to the hockey school. It was rejected! There were several reasons given, but regardless of the statistics you have just heard from the man who turned away my daughter—and his own daughter too—there is still only one real reason: they cannot play because they are girls!

"My daughter and her three brave friends are not the kind of young women who will submit to this kind of injustice. They have gone into hiding to protest this unfair decision and they will not return to their homes until the unjust and sexist decision of the hockey association is revoked!"

Here her voice got very husky and dramatic. "I want my daughter back, but I want her to return in triumph. We have a chance here to accomplish something of great significance, both for today and for the years to come. Give these young crusaders your support! Integrate the hockey school! Let the young women of Amesbury participate in the hockey rinks of our nation!"

It was a pretty dramatic ending and I felt like cheering.

"She's great," said Marna. "She makes me feel like a hero."

"I've heard it all before," sighed Carlie. "She talks the same way when we're trying to decide how to cook our eggs for breakfast."

"I'd rather have her with me than against me," said Steph. "She sure is convincing."

Right away people started calling in to give their opinions. I couldn't believe how many wanted to talk. We had really opened up a hornet's nest.

The first caller was Miss Granby, the phys. ed. teacher. "I think girls should be encouraged to play," she said. "Most of my students are flabby, lazy, and not fit to breed a future generation of healthy Canadians."

Miss Granby wears oxfords and a hair net and has no children. I couldn't imagine anyone ever asking her to breed a Canadian — that shows how far being physically fit gets you.

"I have tried to encourage these girls to play ringette with minimal success," she went on. "The only thing this generation of girls is interested in is boys."

She knows this because she teaches health too. Last year we studied bones and muscles for the third year in a row. We've always tried to get her on to something interesting like dating or sex or marriage, but she keeps telling us that doesn't come until our final year. By then we'll know all about it anyway. That's never made much sense to me.

The next call was from a mother who thought that girls were too delicate to play hockey. She was worried about us damaging our "tender tissue."

Carlie looked confused by that. Marna pointed to her chest to explain.

Then George Benson, who owns the sports store, called in to tell everyone that there was a special line of hockey equipment for women that he would be pleased to carry if girls got to play.

"Good old George," said Steph. "Never misses a chance for some free advertising."

A man who sounded really angry called in to tell everyone that hockey was not ladylike and would teach girls to be aggressive and vicious. Mrs. Klee asked him if he thought it taught boys the same thing.

"No," he replied. "It teaches them sportsmanship."

Kids called in too. I couldn't believe how many of them thought hockey for girls was a good idea. One boy said that it would be more fun to talk to girls if they had an idea of what hockey was all about. One said that if girls started as young as boys do, and worked hard, everyone could play in the same league. Another said that he wouldn't want a girl on his team, but that it would be great to have a girls' hockey league if they could get ice time.

A lot of girls phoned to say they didn't want to play hockey but they didn't see why those who wanted to shouldn't be allowed to. Others said we should play ringette and quite a few thought they wouldn't mind playing hockey.

The calls went on for an hour. By the time it was over I wasn't trying to keep count anymore. The amazing thing was that it was only the adults who thought it was a dumb idea.

There was one call that made me really happy. It was from Bill. "I just wanted to say that I know one of those girls," he said. "She's the kind of person who might have been a good athlete if she'd been given a chance. I hope she gets it."

"Who is that?" asked Carlie.

"I didn't recognize the voice," said Steph. "It's not me. Must be Marna."

"Not me," said Marna.

I said nothing. Bill was dead wrong about my athletic ability, but it was a nice thing for him to say.

Finally the announcer closed the show. "I'd like to thank all the people who called in," he said. "I'm sure that our runaways are listening because they told a friend they could be contacted through this radio station. Your parents are worried, girls. You have made us all aware of the problem. Now I join your families and friends in asking you to please come home, wherever you are."

Then my father came on the air again. "Jane, please come home. Carlie, Steph, Marna, we're worried about all of you. We'll talk this over when we know you're safe. Please come home."

No one spoke as the station switched to music.

I was surprised at the number of people who thought it was a good idea for us to play hockey. I didn't care about Miss Granby or George Benson, but I did care what Bill thought. I'd expected him to be furious about it, but he wasn't. I guess the other girls were thinking the same thing.

Finally Marna broke the silence. "My sister was pretty good, wasn't she?" Jennie had called in to say how proud she was of Marna and how happy she would be when she could play hockey herself.

"She won't be so proud when she sees you on the ice," said Steph. "If you're as vicious as you were today, she won't want to know you."

It didn't take a genius to know what Marna was thinking. All along she'd been feeling bad about Jennie's not being allowed to play hockey when she wanted to so much. "You want to help her out, don't you, Marna?" I said.

"I really don't mind making a fool of myself if it's going to help her do something she really wants. She's a great little kid."

"You know," Steph said slowly, "it's not such a terrible thing that Jane forgot to leave that note. If she hadn't, we never would have known that people don't think it's dumb for us to play hockey."

"I see through you, Steph," cried Carlie. "You don't fool me for a minute. My mother's speech got to you. I was watching you. You *want* to play."

"Well," Steph began, "she sure was convincing and—"

"No," said Carlie. "No! No! No! I won't give in! I won't. I don't care if all the rest of you go home and turn yourselves into Amazons just to make my mother happy. I *won't.*"

"But Belmer is coming for us tonight, Carlie," Marna reminded her. "We have to decide what we're going to do when we leave here."

"Well, I'm not going with him. I didn't make any promises. If you remember, I was asleep at the time."

"But you won't have any choice about leaving. And he's coming to get us in two hours."

"To get *you,* you mean. He'll have to drag me out of here by the ankles. I'm not going to play hockey just to please my mother. She always gets her way, but not this time!"

I couldn't blame Carlie, not really. She had withstood her mother for all those awful days before we ran away. I never could have done it. I knew that, after listening to Mrs. Klee on the radio. Now it would take a miracle — or maybe a small disaster — to get Carlie to give in.

Everybody wins

There seemed no point in talking about it anymore; so we went down to the rink for a game. I think Steph hoped a few hard blows to the head would bring Carlie to her senses.

It was a great game. If we had finished it, I think I would have beaten Marna for the first time. But it kept getting dimmer and dimmer in the arena and harder to see the ball with every shot.

At one point I dug the ball out of the far corner with my stick and passed it down the rink to Carlie. We had an agreement to help each other whenever we could. "Here it comes," I shouted.

"Got it," Carlie replied.

There was an odd flapping sound and then a strange squeal. Carlie hesitated and looked around.

"There's the ball, Carlie," I yelled. "Pass it back to me."

She ran for it, but before she could touch it, it started

moving across the floor. Then, right before my eyes it sprouted wings, lifted off and flew up to the rafters. I looked up. Several dark shapes were swooping down from the ceiling.

"Bats!" Marna screamed.

There may be nothing wrong with bats. Maybe for some people they even make lively pets and pleasant companions, but they paralyse me. I did the only thing I could think of. I fell to the floor and covered my head with my hands. All I could remember was that bats get caught in your hair. The thought of a live bat scratching at my head was so disgusting I started to whimper.

"Jane, Marna, pull yourselves together."

I opened one eye. There was Steph, stick in hand, flailing away at every bat that dared to come close. Till the day I die, that will be my idea of raw courage.

Marna grabbed my hand and the two of us cowered on the floor. Finally Carlie grabbed her stick and jumped up to help Steph. A low-flying bat crashed right into her. She screamed, and they fell to the ice together. Jumping up again, Carlie hit the bat a couple of good wallops with her hockey stick, then went after more.

That left three of us on the floor: Marna, me and the dead bat. The sight of that repulsive thing was all I needed to get me to my feet. I grabbed Marna's arm and we dashed for the exit. Steph and Carlie, hockey sticks swinging, followed us.

We didn't stop running until we were safely in the

lounge. Marna and I collapsed on a sofa, while Steph and Carlie stood laughing and joking about what cowards we had been. Carlie was particularly obnoxious.

"I don't see what's so terrifying about a little thing like a bat."

"I guess it was the surprise more than anything," I said. At that moment I was feeling pretty embarrassed. No one likes to be a coward.

Carlie wouldn't let up. "That's silly. They can't hurt you. I didn't realize you were both such sissies."

I was about to remind her of the vampire bats of South America. I wished one would fly in the window and show her what bats were all about.

But Marna spoke up first. "I know why I'm so frightened of them. My uncle got bitten by one once. He had to have needles for rabies. Twenty-centimetre-long needles. Fourteen of them. In the stomach. How would you like that?"

Carlie went a little pale. "Why? Just because a bat bit him?"

"Bats carry rabies. It's either the needle or you die frothing at the mouth and biting all your friends."

Marna was laying it on a little thick, and she felt bad about it later, but Carlie was really being insufferable. She deserved to be as scared as we had been, but none of us expected her to react so strongly. She turned sheet white and I thought she was going to faint. Instead she sat down and started to cry.

Marna went over to her. "Sorry, Carlie, I didn't mean it. I just don't think anyone should fool around with bats. But you and Steph were really brave."

Carlie just kept crying, her sobs getting louder and louder by the minute.

Steph tried to calm her down. "Never mind, Carlie. It's all over now."

Carlie looked at her through her tears. "Look at my arm." She held it out. There, so tiny they were hard to see, were two sets of tiny pin pricks. "It bit me when it crashed into me. I hardly felt it. But now I'm going to die."

She started to cry again, and now we were all scared too. Steph walked to the door of the lounge. "Jane, get our things packed. Marna, you stay with Carlie. I'll be right back."

In a few minutes she returned with a paper bag in her hand and a determined look on her face. "Let's go, quick," she said.

She led us to the front door and pushed it open. The alarm gave its piercing scream as we stepped out into the dusk. Steph sat down on the steps.

"What are you doing?" asked Marna. "Let's get her to the doctor's right away."

"We're going to the hospital," Steph said. "And the fastest way to get there is in Belmer's squad car."

* * *

Constable Belmer got there in record time. I was so glad to see him, I could even have put up with a few jokes, but he didn't crack a single one. He bundled us all into the squad car and raced off to the hospital with the siren blaring. On the way, he radioed to the police station to tell them to notify our parents and the hospital.

The hospital was ready for us when we got there. They rushed Carlie into Emergency. Steph went with her. She had to, because Carlie wouldn't let go of her hand. In Steph's other hand was the brown paper bag she had been clutching ever since she had led us out the door of the arena.

Marna and I sat down and waited for our parents to arrive. I was a little nervous. I hoped that my mother wouldn't cry or my father shout — or my father cry and my mother shout. I hate scenes. But when they arrived, Mother gave me a big hug. Then Dad did too and said he was glad we were back. No one said a word about hockey.

Marna's parents were doing the same thing, quietly. The Klees were not so quiet. Mrs. Klee was demanding to see her daughter and Mr. Klee was trying to calm her down. Just before things reached all-out hysteria, the doors to the Emergency Ward opened and Carlie, Steph and the doctor walked into the waiting room.

Mrs. Klee gave a terrible shriek and rushed to take

Carlie in her arms. Thinking that her mother believed she was dying of rabies, Carlie smiled calmly and said, "Don't worry, Mother. Steph has saved me."

She held out the paper bag that Steph had been carrying. Mrs. Klee snatched it, looked inside, shrieked again and fainted dead away.

For the next few minutes there was confusion everywhere. Mr. Klee was trying to revive his wife with cold water from a paper cup. The doctor was taking her pulse and my mother was patting her on the hand and calling, "Doris, Doris."

Carlie came over and sat on the bench beside us. She looked very calm for someone at the doors of death.

"What's in the bag?" asked Marna.

"A dead bat," said Carlie with a grin. "I guess I should have warned my mother."

"A dead bat?" said Marna, horrified. "Are you crazy?"

"No," said Carlie. "The doctor says that since we have the bat that bit me they can test it and if it's not rabid, I'm fine. They don't think I need to worry."

"So that's where you went," Marna said, turning to Steph.

"That's right," said Carlie. "She went back down to the rink and got the bat I killed."

We all looked at Steph in amazement. I knew that _I_ couldn't have gone back into that arena for anyone.

Then I thought again. I guess I could have done it for my parents — or for Marna, of course. Or maybe for Bill?

"With friends like that — " said Marna.

"Who cares if they're enemies," I finished.

So Steph did care about Carlie after all. She cared a lot, in spite of the insults. I guess some people just have strange ways of showing their feelings.

When Carlie's mother came to, Carlie apologized for frightening her so. Mrs. Klee was quiet for once. I think she was embarrassed about fainting in front of all those people.

Constable Belmer was still there. Marna's dad went up to him and congratulated him on responding so quickly in an emergency. The rest of our parents did the same. We didn't breathe a word about his finding us the night before. We thought the less said the better.

When I got into the car to go home, I waited for the lecture — but there wasn't one. I thought I should say something, but all I could think of was, "I'm sorry if I upset you."

"We were frantic until last night," said my mother. "Until we knew you were safe."

"How did you know that?"

"We got a phone call from Constable Belmer," my father said. "He told us that you were fine and convinced us that you should be allowed to stay where you were for one more night. He said he'd take care of you."

"That double crosser!"

"Now, Jane," said my mother, "be fair. He didn't bring you home, and we didn't ask him to. But you can hardly blame him for wanting to let us know you were all right. He wouldn't tell us where you were."

"He was very persuasive," said my father. "But he seemed a little confused. He seemed to think you were running away because you *didn't* want to play hockey."

"Hal," said Mother, "this is not the time to talk about that. Let's just be happy that we're all together again."

So we were.

* * *

Allison and Darryl and Bill were waiting on the front lawn when the car pulled in. We went off to the café for cheeseburgers, french fries and milkshakes, and not once did they mention hockey. I think that was Allison's doing.

On the way home I told Bill I had heard him on the radio. He was kind of embarrassed, but said he had meant every word of it. And when we said goodnight, he kissed me — more than once, as a matter of fact.

It was good to be home. When I got upstairs, Allison came into my room and closed the door. "Now what are you going to do?" she asked.

"Nothing," I said. "We heard all those calls on the hot line. I guess ending up with a hockey stick in my hand isn't the worst thing that could happen to me. That's how we spent most of our time in the arena."

She smiled. "You know, I really like the game."

"What do you mean?"

"I play on a team in Chicago. Women's hockey is a big thing there. I love it!"

I guess my mouth dropped open.

"That's right," she went on. "And I'm not a hundred kilos with huge biceps and no front teeth. I'm not vicious either."

"But why didn't you tell me?" I asked.

"I thought you should be allowed to make up your own mind," was all she said.

* * *

It's amazing, the things that happened because we ran away. For example, Mrs. Klee finally admitted to Carlie that she was wrong. Not about hockey, of course — that would have been too much to hope for. But she told Carlie that she'd been wrong to nag her about getting her hair cut, and agreed it looked better long.

That was all Carlie needed to keep her hair short forever. She had a hairdresser repair Steph's job, and by the time school opened in September, she was looking better than she ever had before.

What's more, she seemed to realize that Steph could be right once in a while too. She decided to go on a diet and this time, with a lot of help from Steph, she has stuck to it. Every night after school Steph walks Carlie home. They avoid the Bluebird Café, with its sundaes and milkshakes, and go straight over to the tennis court, where they play till dinner. Carlie is looking better and better. In fact, just last week she had her first name for TATTLE.

Constable Belmer got a citation — for "demonstrating concern for the young citizens of Amesbury above and beyond the call of duty." So now they won't be able to force him to retire. He's already back in form, with a whole raft of new old jokes.

The argument about hockey went on and on. Whenever anyone asked us about it, we just smiled and shrugged. We thought the best thing to do was simply keep our mouths shut and wait to see what would happen.

Eventually the hockey association reached a decision. They would slot ice time for a league for women over twelve. The younger girls would be allowed to enroll in the boys' leagues. Marna's little sister was overjoyed. She rushed right out and bought her equipment. We followed more slowly. We didn't have to play, I guess, but after all the publicity, we thought we should give it a try.

It isn't bad. We aren't very good, and we'll never

make up for all those lost years, but we have a lot of fun — almost as much as we had playing Attack. Since Marna and I play on the same team, I've never made her nose bleed again. I've never stood her up again either, not even for Bill.

She and I often go down to the arena to watch the younger girls play. For some reason, they think we're sort of special. They always come around after their games to tell us how they did. Watching them skate, I sometimes think I was born five years too early. When they're all dressed up in their pads and helmets, you can't tell the boys from the girls.

Maybe that's the way it should be.